LOST SOUL

A Harbinger P.I. Novel

ADAM J. WRIGHT

ALEC HARBINGER, PRETERNATURAL INVESTIGATOR SERIES

LOST SOUL
BURIED MEMORY
DEAD GROUND

CHAPTER 1

THERE ARE SOME DAYS WHEN everything goes okay, or at least as well as you could hope. Then there are other days when it would be better to stay in bed and let the hours drift by while you remain hidden under the blankets.

Today had hardly even started but I already longed to crawl back into bed and pretend the sun had never risen.

In fact, the sun hadn't risen yet. I was standing in my kitchen with a mug of steaming coffee in my hand at five a.m. My lack of sleep and the early hour contributed to my reluctance to face the day ahead but the sinking feeling in the pit of my stomach had more to do with location than time.

I peered out through the dark kitchen window. I could just make out the woods looming in the darkness at the end of the yard. Yep, I was in Dearmont, Maine. So the

1

move from Chicago to this middle-of-nowhere small town by order of the Society hadn't just been a terrible dream.

Here I was, cast away by the Society of Shadows to a quiet town where I "wouldn't do further damage to the Society's image". That was a joke; how could a secret society even have an image to damage?

But the joke was on me because they had banished me to a town where I would be lucky to get a single case. As a preternatural investigator in a world where preternatural beings are hidden from the general population, I hadn't exactly been overrun with cases in Chicago so I expected to be doing nothing more than sitting on my ass most days in Dearmont.

The problem with that was that the Society wouldn't put up with me for much longer if my monthly reports said nothing more than "no activity". I wouldn't just be sitting on my ass: I would be out on it. And from the rumors I'd heard, nobody left the Society of Shadows and stayed alive for very long afterward.

I took a sip of coffee and grimaced at the bitter taste. Leaning against the sink, I surveyed the kitchen and told myself that this was my home now so I had better get used to it and find a case sooner rather than later.

The house was still unfamiliar to me because the first time I saw it was yesterday after driving here from Bangor airport. The Society had arranged to have my Land Rover transported to Bangor from Chicago, so I could use it as soon as I landed, and they had also had my boxed belongings brought to the new house.

But their insistence on controlling every aspect of the move meant that they had chosen the house I was to live in, as well as the office I was to work out of in town. Sure, they took care of the first three months rent for both places but that was small compensation for having to move into a house I hadn't chosen myself.

As things had turned out, the house was actually quite nice. Located on a seemingly quiet tree-lined street of fairly large four and five bedroom dwellings, my own four-bedroom home was more than spacious enough, even with my boxes cluttering up the living room and two of the bedrooms.

I hadn't unpacked anything but the bare essentials yet but I knew that even after I'd emptied all the boxes, the belongings that had filled my two-bedroom apartment in Chicago would be lost in this spacious house. Well, that was the way it was going to have to be. I couldn't afford new furniture unless I found paying clients.

And in this small town, that might prove to be an impossible task.

I finished the coffee and put the empty cup into the sink. Outside, a gray pre-dawn light was seeping into the sky. Summer was just beginning so I expected the day to get hot later. I cranked up the air in the house so the place would be cool when I returned. If things were as slow as I expected at the office, I might even close up early and come back here this afternoon. No need to put in long hours on my first day on the job.

I'd seen a barbecue in the yard when I'd arrived yesterday. Maybe if I grabbed a few beers at the local store later, along with some burgers, I could treat myself to a quiet house-warming party in the sun.

I went upstairs, showered, and dressed in jeans and a flannel shirt. By the time I came back downstairs, the darkness beyond the windows had been replaced by a bright gray. The uppermost branches of the fir and elm trees in the wood had caught a sliver of orange sunlight but the shadows beneath were still dark and mysterious.

I put on my boots, grabbed the keyring that held my house, car, and office keys from a small table near the front door, and went out onto the driveway. There was a slight breeze, cool against my skin and carrying a fresh earthy scent with an overtone of sharp pine. I was a world away from the exhaust-laden air of Chicago.

The other houses on the street were mostly dark. A few lights shone behind closed curtains but most of the houses were dark shapes against the early dawn light.

I climbed into the Land Rover and started the engine. It roared to life, shattering the dawn stillness. A few more lights came on along the street, as the noise awoke the neighbors. I could imagine them peering out from their bedroom windows and cursing "that guy who moved in yesterday".

Sorry, folks, I don't intend to get up this early every day. It's just that trying to sleep in a strange house doesn't work for me. Once you get to know me, you'll see I'm really a great guy, a perfect neighbor. I keep myself to myself and never bring my work home with me, which is a good thing since my work involves demons and vampires.

I backed out of the driveway and headed toward town, consulting the map of Dearmont on the passenger seat. The map showed Main Street and my office was circled in red marker. I'd been told the office was located next to a donut shop, so it had that going for it at least.

Ten minutes and two wrong turns later, I found Main Street. It was a long road lined with two and three level buildings housing businesses like the general store, a bookshop, an outdoor store, and a number of restaurants and eating establishments. Only the general store was open at the moment, the rest of the buildings dark and quiet.

I found the donut shop, a place imaginatively called Dearmont Donuts, and spotted a narrow door next to it with the words HARBINGER P.I. printed in black letters on the frosted glass. I frowned when I saw that there was light spilling out through the glass onto the sidewalk. I slowed the Land Rover and bent forward to check the windows above Dearmont Donuts. The lights were on up there too. Maybe someone had left them on by mistake.

I found a parking space around the back of the building and locked the Land Rover before walking around to the door that bore my name. On impulse, I tried the door before using my key.

It opened.

So not only had someone left the lights burning, they'd also left the door unlocked. Sighing, I stepped inside and found myself in a small foyer with a steep flight of stairs leading up to the next floor. The foyer was empty except for a wooden business card holder on the wall filled with cards. I took one and inspected it.

The card was black and in gold lettering it read ALEC HARBINGER P.I. (PRETERNATURAL INVESTIGATOR) DISCRETION ASSURED. Below that, there was a phone number that I assumed belonged to a phone in the office upstairs.

I ascended the narrow stairs and found myself in a wood-paneled hallway with three doors. Two of the doors had frosted glass panes. The third, the door closest to me, was solid wood and had a gold plaque that said BATHROOM. That was good to know because I intended to be drinking a lot of coffee here.

The door at the far end of the hallway had my name printed in the same lettering as the entrance door downstairs. The other door, situated halfway between the bathroom and my office, intrigued me the most because its glass pane displayed the word ASSISTANT. Not only that, there was a strong smell of coffee and baked goods emanating from the room beyond.

The door was ajar. I pushed it all the way open and was greeted by the sight of a woman fussing around a coffee maker. She wore a white blouse, black pencil skirt, and thick-rimmed glasses. She was slim and tall, her height accentuated by the fact that her dark hair was piled up on top of her head. She turned to face me and I guessed her age to be mid-twenties.

"Mr. Harbinger," she said, putting down the coffee pot. She had a British accent. "You're here."

"I am indeed," I said. "This is my office after all. You can call me Alec, by the way. And you are?"

"Felicity Lake," she said, coming forward with her hand outstretched.

We shook. Her hand was warm, her grip light.

"Would you like a coffee?" she asked. "And an apple bake? I have apple bakes. I made them myself this morning." She returned to the coffee maker and began pouring from the pot into a cup. There was a frenetic energy about her that might come from nervousness or could just be a part of her personality. It was difficult to be sure.

She handed me the cup of coffee. "Cream and one sugar, just the way you like it."

So the Society had told her how I took my coffee. That was very thorough of them. What else had they told her about me?

"Thanks, Felicity. And I would love to try one of those apple bakes." I gestured to the plate of golden brown goodies that smelled mouth-wateringly of apple and cinnamon.

"Of course!" She went over to the plate and began transferring some of the bakes onto a smaller dish. As well as my coffee preference, the Society must have told her about my love of sweets and any food that was bad for me.

"I'll bring these to your office for you," she offered.

"Thanks," I said, turning and heading for my office door. Felicity followed, the aroma of the apple bakes filling the hallway.

My office was spacious even with the large dark wood desk sitting by the window. A large leather chair sat behind the desk with two smaller chairs for clients on the opposite side. A computer sat on the desk, as well as an intercom device that I assumed connected to Felicity's office. The floor had a thick, pale-green carpet and the walls were painted a similar color. A bookshelf ran along one wall with leather-bound grimoires and lore books sitting on it.

"The books are from your old office in Chicago," Felicity said, placing the dish of apple bakes on my desk. "And that's your old trash basket too." She pointed to a wire basket on the floor beneath the window.

I sat in the big chair and swiveled it to face the window and the view of Main Street.

"I'll get everything ready for your first client," Felicity said.

"I have a client?" I tried not to sound too surprised but failed miserably.

"Yes," she said, smoothing down her skirt with her hands. "She'll be here at nine." She turned to leave.

"Felicity," I said, stopping her.

Turning to face me, she asked, "Yes, Alec?"

I looked into her dark eyes and said, "Were you sent here to spy on me?"

CHAPTER 2

SHE SAGGED SLIGHTLY AGAINST THE door frame. "Oh dear. I didn't mean to … I've made a mess of this, haven't I?" She leaned more heavily against the frame and I wondered if she was going to faint. I rushed over to her and took her hand and shoulder, guiding her to one of the client chairs by the desk. Felicity was shaking her head and looking at the floor with tears in her eyes. She kept mumbling, "I can't believe I'm so stupid."

"Take a seat," I said, pushing her gently into the chair. I sat on the edge of the desk. "Would you like a drink of water or something?"

She shook her head, still staring at the green carpet. "I'll be fine in a minute." Then she looked up at me with watery eyes and said, "I'm sorry."

"Hey, don't worry about it. You were just doing what you were told to do. I don't hold it against you."

"What gave me away?" she asked.

"Well, first, there's the fact that I've never had an assistant before. I didn't have one in Chicago, so I doubt the Society would think I'm going to need one working this small town. Then there's your accent. You're obviously from England, so that probably means you were sent here from the London headquarters. Why do I warrant an assistant all the way from headquarters? The answer is, I don't."

Felicity nodded slowly.

"And another thing," I said. "Since you're from London, I'm willing to bet that you were sent here by my father."

She nodded again. "I was assigned to you by the Inner Circle but I was to report to your father directly, yes." A tear rolled down her left cheek. When she spoke again, her voice cracked slightly. "This is my first assignment and I've ballsed everything up on my first day. The Society will kick me out." She began to cry softly.

I hate it when people cry in front of me. I never know what to do and that makes me feel uncomfortable and helpless. "Hey, hey, there's no need to cry," I said softly. "I'll find you a tissue." I left the room and went into Felicity's office, where I found a box of Kleenex on her desk. When I returned, she had composed herself and was sitting up straight. Her eyes were still leaking, though.

11

I handed her the box of tissues.

"Thank you, Mr. Harbinger," she said, dabbing at her eyes. "I'm very sorry to have done this to you. I was only following orders. Now, I must return to London and inform the Inner Circle of my failure to carry out my duties." She got up and walked toward the door.

"Hey, wait," I said. "You haven't done anything to me except give me coffee and apple bakes." I took a bite of one of the bakes. The sweet apple and cinnamon filling melted on my tongue. I said, "They're delicious, by the way."

She smiled, but there was still a look of despair in her eyes.

"Come and sit down," I suggested. "We can talk about this."

Slowly, she came back into the office and took a seat. "I really don't know what there is to talk about, Mr. Harbinger."

"I told you, call me Alec," I said. I was going to add that old line, "Mr. Harbinger is my father," but decided against it, since she knew my father and he was the reason she was in trouble right now.

Felicity threw her arms up in an exaggerated shrug. "It doesn't really matter anymore, Alec. Our working relationship is over. When the Society finds out I failed to stay undercover, they'll recall me to London."

"Maybe," I said. "But first they have to find out. Besides, there's no way the Inner Circle could think I wouldn't figure out that you were here to spy on me. I think this is more a case of them letting me know that they're watching me, in case I screw up again."

She frowned at me. "Screw up again?"

"Oh, they didn't tell you why you were spying on me in the first place? They didn't mention Paris?"

Her frown deepened. "Paris, France?"

I nodded. "If they didn't mention it to you, don't worry about it." I certainly wasn't in the mood to go over all that again. I'd spent more than enough time explaining it to the Inner Circle under interrogation a few months ago.

"I don't know anything about Paris," she said. "I was just told to come and work for you and send a report to headquarters once a month, or more often, if you behaved strangely."

I nodded. Yeah, that figured. It seemed to me that the Inner Circle, led by my father, had decided to use Felicity Lake as a pawn in a game that was being played between them and me. Even I didn't know what that game was. As far as I was concerned, I'd been questioned about the events in Paris and demoted from my office in Chicago to the sleepy town of Dearmont. I thought that was the end of the matter, but the fact they'd sent someone to spy on me suggested otherwise.

"Felicity," I asked her, "how good of an assistant are you?"

She looked at me with a glint of pride in her moist eyes. "I'm very good. I've been through the Society's three-year course and I was hoping to become an investigator like yourself. As you know, that requires at least a year working with a fully-fledged investigator."

"Ah," I said, understanding now. "And that's how they sold you this job. They told you that the time you spent working with me, and spying on the side, would count toward your time in the field."

She nodded.

"Here's the thing," I said. "Through no fault of your own, you've been dragged into this game the Society are playing with me. Now, we both know that your cover has been blown, but the people who sent you here don't know that. So, if you still want to be my assistant and spend time in the field, that's fine with me."

Her eyes widened and a small smile spread across her mouth. "Really? But what about sending reports to your father?"

I shrugged. "Send them as normal. I don't expect much to happen around here anyhow."

Felicity's hand flew to her mouth and her eyes shot to the clock on the wall. "Mrs. Robinson!"

"Mrs. Robinson?" I had no idea what she was talking about.

"Your client. She'll be here soon. I have to get everything ready."

I followed her eyes to the clock. It wasn't even eight yet. "I thought you said she was coming at nine."

"She is," she said, getting up.

"So she won't be here for another hour."

"Still, I need to prepare the reception area and make more coffee. And fix my makeup."

"Okay," I said. I guess I couldn't blame her for being nervous on her first day. "So you go do that and I'll hang around in here."

She nodded and scuttled to the door. Before she went out, she turned back to me and said, "Thank you."

Before I could reply, she disappeared into the hallway.

I sat in the big leather chair behind the desk and swiveled the seat from side to side a few times, surveying my new office. It would take me some time, but I could probably get used to this place. Rolling the chair over to the window, I peered out at Main Street. The sun was up now and the street was busy with people opening up their businesses or just strolling along the sidewalk. Some of them had rolled newspapers tucked under their arms and takeout coffee in their hands.

Bringing my own coffee and the apple bakes over to the window, I ate breakfast and watched Dearmont come to life. That might be overstating things. Sure, the traffic increased and a few townsfolk wandered along the sidewalk, but this was hardly Chicago. I wondered what preternatural problem Mrs. Robinson could possibly have in a place like this.

Obviously I knew enough not to judge the town by its outward appearance; dark secrets and creatures sometimes lurk in the most innocent looking places. But I can usually sense those things and Dearmont not only looked like a sleepy town, it felt like it to my innermost senses, too. Sure, there could be a haunted house somewhere in the area, maybe even a ghoul or two at the cemetery (those damned things got everywhere), but I had a hunch that Dearmont was a dead zone as far as preternatural activity went.

I really needed to stop trusting in my hunches so much.

CHAPTER 3

I SPENT THE NEXT HOUR on my computer, checking the local news reports on the net. Maybe whatever Mrs. Robinson wanted to hire me for was connected to an event that had been reported somewhere. But my search seemed pointless. The last time Dearmont had made the news was when a local librarian named Deirdre Summers had gone missing and was presumed dead after her clothing had been found on the shore of the lake near town. That had been three years ago.

Still, I grabbed a notebook from the small pile Felicity had put on my desk and made a couple of notes. The sheriff investigating the case was Sheriff John Cantrell. A picture showed him standing by the edge of the lake, staring out over the water with a searching look in his eyes.

He'd probably been told to adopt that expression by the photographer.

Cantrell was a big man and looked like he might spend his free time wrestling grizzlies for fun. But it was the deputy standing next to him who caught my attention. She was stunningly attractive.

She was much smaller than Cantrell, but who wasn't? Her hair was cut to shoulder length and was a fiery red color. It framed a face that wouldn't be out of place on the cover of a magazine, with high cheekbones and cat-like green eyes.

Despite her model's face, she wasn't thin, but had curves in all the right places. Even her uniform couldn't hide those curves. Standing with her hands on her hips, she also stared out over the lake, but her face looked more thoughtful than her boss's. I guessed she was the brains and he was the brawn of the local law.

I searched for her name, but it wasn't mentioned either beneath the photo or in the article.

Apart from the missing woman case, which made national news, Dearmont wasn't considered interesting by journalists. The only other mentions of the town on the net were uploads of articles written for the Dearmont Observer, the local paper. Most of these were written by someone named Wesley Jones, who I assumed was the town's reporter. The articles covered events like a bake sale at the church, the 4th of July parade, and the Christmas parade. The people here sure seemed to like their parades.

I reached over to the intercom device on my desk and pressed the button. Felicity's voice came out of the speaker a few seconds later. "Yes, Alec?"

"Do we know why Mrs. Robinson wants to hire us?" Maybe I should have just asked Felicity in the first place and saved myself the time I'd just spent looking at articles about coffee mornings and town council meetings. Still, if I'd done that, I wouldn't have seen the picture of the stunning redheaded deputy by the lake.

"No idea," she said. "Should I have asked her when she called to make an appointment?"

"No, sometimes people don't like to talk about this kind of stuff until they're here in the office." I paused and then said, "When did Mrs. Robinson call?"

"Yesterday."

"You were here yesterday?"

"Yes, I've been here two weeks. I had to oversee the refurbishment of the offices and unpack your books and trash can. I also put an advertisement in the local newspaper last week. That's probably where Mrs. Robinson heard about us."

"Okay," I said. "I just hope she isn't a kook." I released the button and sat back in my chair. It was entirely possible that Mrs. Robinson was one of the many people who came through the doors of preternatural investigators' offices with either a crazy story or a ridiculous request. I'd heard it all during my time in the field. Aliens are abducting my dog. Elvis lives in my garden shed. The award for the craziest story I ever heard goes to an old woman in Chicago who told me that her cat was planning to assassinate the president.

It comes with the territory, of course. My job is to take cases where there might be some kind of preternatural activity. That means I deal with vampires, demons, faeries, werewolves, and a whole host of other creatures that most people don't believe in. Some of the people who *do* believe in those creatures are not always of sound mind.

Those people are turned away once we realize their case isn't a genuine haunting, possession, curse, or whatever.

The other potential clients we have to turn away are those that think the P.I. stands for Private Investigator and not Preternatural Investigator. There's a preternatural investigator office in almost every city and large town across America and Europe—hell, there's even one in Dearmont, Maine now—so you'd think people would know who we are and what we do, even if they think we're nuts.

But they still come and ask us to follow a cheating spouse or track down a long lost family member. I usually keep contact details of local private investigators so I can pass the customers on once I realize their problems aren't preternaturally based.

Mrs. Robinson could be a kook, or someone in need of a private eye. Or maybe she had a real preternatural problem. I had to speak to her and find out, but I wasn't counting my expenses checks just yet.

The intercom buzzed and Felicity's voice said, "Mrs. Robinson is here, Alec."

"Send her in," I said. "And Felicity, you come in, too. You can take notes if you like."

A couple of seconds later, the door opened and an elegantly-dressed woman in her fifties entered. I got up and went around the desk, my hand out. "Mrs. Robinson, I'm Alec Harbinger."

She shook my hand with a soft grip and said, "Please, call me Amelia."

"Of course. Take a seat." I gestured to the chairs in front of the desk and she took the one where Felicity had been crying earlier.

Felicity came in and closed the door behind her. She was carrying a legal pad and a pen. I pulled the other client seat halfway around the desk so that Felicity wasn't sitting next to Amelia Robinson. I didn't want the older woman to feel crowded. Some of our clients only come to us after they've reached a point of desperation regarding their situation. Talking about things you've been told aren't real isn't always easy, and I wanted Mrs. Robinson to feel comfortable.

Felicity took the seat and sat poised with her pen above the legal pad.

I looked at Amelia Robinson. From the pearls around her neck, perfectly coiffed gray hair, and expensive-looking blue blouse, black pants, and black high-heels, I guessed she was a successful businesswoman or a member of a rich family who made some wise investments.

"How can I help you today?" I asked her, sitting down.

"I have a … problem," she said. Her voice was controlled and even, supporting my theory of businesswoman. I could imagine her talking to a board of directors with that voice. "But before we begin, I must be assured of your discretion. I am well-known in Maine society and I cannot abide a scandal."

I frowned. "And by scandal, you mean…." I let my voice trail off, waiting for her to finish my sentence.

"I mean hiring you," she said. "Talking to you. Being here in your office. If word got out that I had hired a supernatural detective, I'd be the laughing stock of the East Coast."

So, at least she wasn't here under the mistaken belief that I was a mundane private investigator. I was also pretty sure she wasn't a kook, but I wouldn't know for sure until I heard her story.

"As it says on my card," I said, "discretion is assured. We're very aware of the delicate nature of our work and we act accordingly."

"Very well." She looked around the office as if she were an army sergeant inspecting the privates' quarters. I hadn't had time to settle in yet, so at least the place was still tidy. "It isn't like I have a choice," she said, her gaze resting on me.

"Tell me all about it," I said, sitting back in my seat, my body language telling her I was ready to listen.

"It's our son, James. He's nineteen and something has happened to him. Something terrible." Her level tone cracked slightly and she reached into her purse for a tissue. She wasn't crying yet, but maybe she knew that the story she was about to tell always made her break down at a certain point in its telling.

I glanced at Felicity. She was scribbling notes.

"Just take your time," I told Amelia. "There's no hurry. What's your husband's name?"

"George," she said. "George Robinson."

Felicity wrote the name down.

"We own Robinson-Lubecki Lumber," Amelia went on. "When we met thirty years ago, George was working for his father in a little company called Robinson Lumber. I was in charge of the Maine expansion of my own father's company, Lubecki Lumber."

"Is Lubecki your maiden name?" I asked.

She nodded. "When our business expanded, George's father, Harold Robinson, and my father went into competition with one another and it wasn't pretty, to say the least. But George and I saw past all that. We fell in love with each other, despite our family's feuding."

I really didn't need to hear her Romeo and Juliet life story, so I said, "Since the company is now called Robinson-Lubecki Lumber, I'm assuming it all turned out well in the end."

"Yes," she said. "After our fathers died, we married and merged the two companies into one of the largest lumber businesses on the East Coast."

"All's well that ends well," I said.

"Except it hasn't ended well. Something has happened to James." Her eyes got watery and she dabbed at them with the tissue.

"Okay, tell me about that. What do you think has happened to him?"

"To understand that fully, you would have to know what James was like before. George and I made sure our son never wanted for anything. We spoiled him from the day he was born. As a result, James grew up feeling privileged and entitled. He was the epitome of a rich brat, living off his trust fund, partying, and dating a string of women. He drank sometimes, and we suspected he was using drugs, but he was never hostile toward me or his father."

"And that all changed one day?" I asked.

"Yes," she said, nodding. "In early April, James and some of his friends went up to Dark Rock Lake for a weekend. There are cabins up there and I suppose it's a perfect place for parties. You know, plenty of booze, loud music, and girls."

"Yeah, I know," I said.

"When he came back from Dark Rock Lake, James was like a different person. He lost interest in going anywhere. We always used to travel to New York as a family twice a year, and we had a trip scheduled the week after James returned from the lake, but he refused to travel with us. That wasn't like him. He always loved our New York trips." Her eyes drifted away as if she were reminiscing about past vacations.

"Is that it?" I asked, bringing her back to the present. "He didn't want to go to New York?"

"No, of course not," Amelia replied, shaking her head and frowning at me. "What do you think I am, some crazy old lady? James refusing to go to New York was just the start. There were other changes, too. He began asking about the financial arrangements we had set up if George and I should die."

"Your wills," I said.

"Yes, and also how our company shares would be allocated between him and Georgia."

"Georgia?" Felicity asked. She had already filled one page of the legal pad with writing and was moving on to a second.

"Our daughter," Amelia said.

"James's sister?" I asked.

"Yes, of course."

"Younger or older?"

"Georgia is his younger sister. She's eighteen next month."

"Is Georgia James's only sibling?" I asked.

Amelia nodded.

I leaned forward in my chair. "So how is the family fortune split between James and Georgia?"

She looked shocked at the question. "Is that relevant?"

"It might be."

"Everything is split down the middle. They each get fifty percent of all money and assets, as well as equal shares of controlling interest in Robinson-Lubecki Lumber."

"Okay, so you think James is taking an unhealthy interest in the family fortune and he doesn't want to go to New York."

"It isn't only New York. He hardly leaves the house now. It used to be that he would disappear with his friends for days. Now, he just stays home. Sometimes he goes walking in the woods around our house, but I don't think he's gone any farther than that since he came back from the lake party. I've spoken to George about it and he says James is just going through a phase. If he knew I'd come to see you about this, he'd tell me I was crazy."

"You're not crazy," I told her. "You're a mother who's concerned for her son. But why did you come to see me and not a normal private eye? I'm not seeing a preternatural angle here."

She looked at me with worried eyes and said, "I'm afraid that James might be … possessed."

I sat back again, body language open, giving her the subconscious signal that I was ready to listen to whatever she said next without judgement. "Go on," I said gently.

"Well, for one thing, he's become nocturnal," Amelia said. "He only seems to come out at night. That's when he goes walking in the woods. During the daytime, he stays in his room." She paused and then asked, "Do you think he's a vampire?"

"It doesn't sound like vampirism," I said. "He'd be doing more than walking around the woods at night, he'd be going into town in search of prey. Does he eat normally?"

"He raids the fridge, if that's what you mean. For him, that's always been normal."

"And you've seen him eating the food from the fridge?"

She nodded. "Yes."

"Vampires don't eat," I told her. "They're sustained by the blood of their victims."

"Then … a demon?" She looked even more worried.

"I don't know," I said. "I'm not even sure this is a preternatural case. Your husband could be right and this might be nothing more than a nineteen-year-old kid going through a phase. But the nocturnal wandering in the woods does give me enough reason to investigate. I might find that there's no preternatural connection at all, and then I'll have to drop the case. But for now, I'm willing to take a look."

Amelia smiled thinly. "Thank you."

"I'll need to come to your house," I said. "And I may bring my assistant along. We'll need to talk to James and take a look at those woods."

I saw a slight smile cross Felicity's face at the prospect of going out into the field. To me, the case sounded mundane. There was barely enough strangeness about it to suggest there was even a slim chance of preternatural activity. But beggars can't be choosers, and at the moment, Amelia Robinson's case was all I had. It might be the only case to come through this office for a while, so there was nothing to lose by investigating it.

"I have to remind you," Amelia said, "about being discreet. Especially where my husband is concerned. He has no idea I came here today, no idea about who you are or what you do."

"We probably won't need to speak with him," I said. "The important thing is that we speak with James and investigate the woods."

"That's fine," Amelia said.

"Excellent," I said, standing. "Now, Felicity will take you to her office where she'll explain our fees and take some more details from you. We'll need your address, of course, and the names of the people James went to Dark Rock Lake with, if you know any of them. I assume you'd like us to start immediately?"

She nodded. "Yes, please."

"Then we'll see you at your house later today." I held out my hand and she shook it. Her grip was a little stronger than it had been when she's arrived and I wondered if that was because she felt more confident now that she had confided in someone. I doubted she had told her husband that she was afraid James might be a vampire.

"Thank you, Mr. Harbinger," she said as Felicity led her out of the office.

"Glad to help," I said, and closed the door after they'd left. I sat behind the desk and did an internet search for Dark Rock Lake. It was fifty miles north of Dearmont and seemed to be a typical summer vacation destination with cabins on the lakeshore and wildlife trails winding through the woods.

"What happened to you while you were there, James?" I whispered as I scrolled through photos of the lake and cabins. The place looked innocent enough. I was probably going to have to go there at some point if I discovered something preternatural in James's case.

Twenty minutes later, Felicity came back into the office. She had a smile on her face. "Mrs. Robinson paid us for a week and five hundred dollars to cover expenses."

"Let's not spend it all yet," I said. "We might end up giving her most of that money back."

Her face fell. "You don't think this is a preternatural matter?"

I sighed. "I think this one should be known as The Case of the Moody Teenager."

"Well, it might be more than just that," she said hopefully. "Maybe James Robinson is demon-possessed or something."

I raised an eyebrow. "You make it sound like you want the poor guy to need saving. We'll check it out, but don't get your hopes up. I know you want your first case to be exciting, but this one really looks like James is just being a typical teenager."

"But he's staying in his room all day."

I shrugged. "Maybe he's trying to avoid someone. He might have had an argument with someone at that lake party."

"He only goes out at night and he wanders the woods," she said.

"Maybe he's discovered Goth music and he's exploring his tortured soul."

Her eyes lit up. "Tortured by...."

"Not tortured by a demon," I cut in.

"What, then?"

"Tortured by Goth music."

She rolled her eyes. "Don't you think this could be a preternatural case? Isn't there even a slim chance?"

"Sure there is," I said. "That's why we're going to check it out."

"Great. So what's our first move?"

"First, we talk to the people who went to that party, then we go see James Robinson."

"Okay," Felicity said. "Mrs. Robinson only gave me one name when I asked her who was at that party. She said she doesn't know all of her son's acquaintances, but there's one guy who was definitely at that party: Leon Smith, James's best friend."

"Do we have an address for him?"

She nodded. "Address and phone number." That was good. Felicity had been thorough getting the information from Amelia Robinson.

"So, let's give him a call and arrange a meet."

"The number is in my office," she said, going to the door. "I'll call him from the office phone in there." She left and I got out of my chair went over to the window. Main Street was buzzing with people now. Maybe Dearmont wasn't so sleepy after all.

"Leon Smith is at home," Felicity called out from her office.

"Is he willing to talk to us?"

"Yeah, I told him we were private detectives and we wanted to ask him some questions about the party at Dark Rock Lake."

"What did he say?" I asked as I left my office and shut the door. I stood in the hallway, watching Felicity as she set the answering machine on the phone and grabbed her purse from where it had been hanging on the back of her chair.

"He said, and I quote, 'Sure, that was a weird-ass party.' He sounded more than willing to answer a few questions. He lives a few miles out of town. Do you have GPS?"

"Yeah, I've got a portable GPS in the Land Rover."

"Weapons?"

I frowned at her. "We're going to question someone, not attack a nest of vampires. We won't need weapons."

As we walked down the stairs, she said, "The Society of Shadows Investigative Guidebook say that an investigator should be armed at all times. You never know when you might be attacked. At the very least, you should have a dagger, preferably enchanted, and you should also...."

"Yeah, there's some stuff in the car," I told her as we left the building and I locked the door. The day was really warming up. The delicious smell of donuts drifted from the shop next door.

"Don't you have any weapons on your person?" Felicity asked.

"No," I said. "I only got here yesterday and I didn't think it would be a good idea to take an enchanted dagger through airport security."

She followed me to the back of the building where the Land Rover was parked. I could sense that she wanted to say something more to me regarding my lack of weapons.

"What is it?" I asked her as I climbed into the driver's seat and she was getting in the passenger side. I swept the map of Dearmont off her seat and onto the floor so she wouldn't sit on it.

She didn't say anything until she was settled in the seat and I had started the engine. Then she said, "I've noticed you have a lack of regard for the rules and regulations of the Society."

"Oh, really?" I said. "Well, the Society have a lack of regard for me, so that makes us even."

She sighed and looked out of her window, but she didn't say anything.

"If you're not happy about how I run my business," I said as I backed out of the parking space, "write it in a report and send it to my father."

CHAPTER 4

FELICITY DIDN'T SPEAK TO ME as we hit Main Street. I said to her, "The GPS is by your feet." I turned right and began driving north, but I had no idea where I was going.

She found the GPS, picked it up, unwound the tangled power wire, and plugged it into the cigarette lighter. After keying in our destination, she stuck the GPS to the windshield. It computed our route and the female voice told me to turn around. I was going the wrong way.

The street wasn't really busy so I made a U turn and headed in the other direction.

"Are you going to keep bringing up the reason I was sent here?" she asked quietly. Even though her voice was low, there was an angry edge to it.

"I'm sorry," I said. "I didn't mean to bring my father into it. It's just that at the moment, I feel like I've been shafted by the Society. I had a good business going in Chicago and they shipped me here, away from all that. It makes me angry."

"Well, that isn't my fault," she said. "Whatever you did in Paris must have been pretty bad for them to banish you from your old job, your old life."

I looked at her and gave her a thin smile. "They could have done much worse." I decided to tell her what was really playing on my mind regarding my enforced relocation. "Look, here's the thing. When I was in Chicago, I did a lot of good and helped a lot of people. Now that I'm here in Dearmont, I just don't think I'll be able to do that anymore. Not on the same scale, anyway."

Felicity's anger seemed to soften slightly. Her voice was much gentler when she said, "You must really miss Chicago."

"Yeah, I do. I have friends there; people I can rely on. I've trusted them with my life on many occasions and they've never disappointed me. Here," I gestured through the window at Main Street, "I don't know anyone."

"That will change in time, Alec. You just need to settle in your new environment. And I know we got off to a shaky start, but maybe someday, you'll trust me like you do your old friends."

I shrugged. I wasn't going to commit to anything. We left Main Street and followed a road that took us south. We drove through a residential area where the houses looked like they might date back to the late nineteenth century, then took a narrow highway that cut through the dense wood that virtually encircled Dearmont.

That was when I noticed the car behind us.

It was a dark green Ford Taurus that seemed unremarkable, except that I was sure it had been behind us when I was driving north along Main Street and then had followed us again after I'd turned south.

It had always been a couple of cars behind us, hanging back as we'd made our way through town. Now it was directly behind us because there were no other cars on the highway.

"We have company," I told Felicity.

At first, she frowned, not understanding what I meant. Then she turned in her seat and looked out of the rear window. "Are they following us?"

"Maybe." I squinted at the rearview mirror. There seemed to be two men in the car, the driver and a passenger in the front.

"What are we going to do?" Felicity whispered as if the men in the car might hear her if she spoke at a normal level.

I looked at the digital map on the GPS screen. There was a side road up ahead, on the left. If I took that road and the Taurus followed, that would confirm we were being tailed. It wouldn't explain why, though.

As I was trying to think of reasons someone would want to follow us, the Taurus accelerated, looming larger in the Land Rover's rear window. Then it cut left and began to overtake us.

I had a bad feeling about this.

The Taurus came level with us and I glanced over at the driver. He was a thin man with short-cropped black hair and a goatee, wearing a black sweater. His passenger was burlier, with a full beard and a black sweater to match the driver's.

The driver shot me a grin that looked both amused and wicked at the same time. I noticed that his window was fully open. Steering with his right hand, he lifted his left to the open window. He was holding a gun, its muzzle pointed at the front tire of the Land Rover.

I hit the brakes hard. The tires squealed on the road as we skidded to a stop. Felicity screamed as she shot forward in her seat, but the seatbelt prevented her from flying through the windshield.

My own seatbelt constricted across my chest, driving the air out of my lungs.

Up ahead, the Taurus skidded into a U-turn so that it was facing us. The maneuver was executed perfectly. These guys were good.

"Hold on," I told Felicity as I floored the accelerator pedal.

We lurched forward and I steered around the Taurus, which was still picking up speed after its sudden change of direction.

In the rearview mirror, I saw the Taurus turn around again, white smoke belching from its tires as they sought purchase on the road. We were never going to be able to outrun it.

My mind was racing. If we were going to get out of this alive, we needed to fight back. "Take the wheel," I told Felicity.

"What?"

"Take the wheel. I need to get into the back."

She swallowed and nodded. "Okay."

I put the stick shift into neutral so the Land Rover wouldn't stall and clambered into the back seat. Felicity slid over and took the wheel, slamming the vehicle into gear again and putting her foot on the gas. I thanked the stars that she was English; she knew how to drive a stick shift.

I glanced out of the rear window. The Taurus was close and gaining on us. I could see the grim look of determination in the dark eyes of the driver.

Reaching under the seat, I found what I wanted. I pulled the long, cloth-wrapped bundle onto the back seat and began to unwrap it, pulling at the silk ties that held the cloth in place.

Felicity glanced back at me. "What's that?"

"I told you I had weapons in the car." The cloth fell aside and I grasped the hilt of the broadsword. As soon as it was in my hand, the rune-inscribed blade began to flicker with blue flame. This was no ordinary flame. If touched to paper, it wouldn't set it alight. The light that pulsated around the sword was cold, brilliant, magical energy. The weapon was enchanted.

"Slow down," I told Felicity.

She sounded worried. "Are you sure? They're already right behind us." The blue glow from the sword illuminated her dark eyes.

"If you don't slow down, it's going to make what I'm about to do next even more dangerous than it already is."

"Okay," she said. "Slowing down." She pressed the brake gently. Our speed barely changed.

"Faster," I said.

"Faster? I thought you wanted me to slow down." She hit the gas again.

"No, I mean press the brake faster. Make us go slower."

She nodded and slowed us again. This time, the deceleration threw me against the back of her seat.

The Taurus came alongside us again.

"Hit the brakes hard," I shouted to Felicity.

She did and the Land Rover juddered to a halt. The Taurus shot past us. It skidded to a stop and began to turn to face us.

I opened my door and threw myself out of the Land Rover. As soon as my boots hit the road, I sprinted toward the Taurus, sword in hand.

Before the dark green car could accelerate again, I jumped up onto its hood and drove the sword through the metal to the engine beneath. The enchanted blade slid easily through the engine, disabling it. The Taurus emitted a metallic squeal and then died as if it were a monster that I'd stabbed through the heart.

The bearded guy in the passenger seat had a shotgun. He leaned out of his window and took aim, trying to shoot me off the hood of the car. Before he pulled the trigger, I leaped up onto the roof of the Taurus, out of his sight. The shotgun discharged, the sudden explosion of sound disturbing a flock of birds in a nearby tree and sending them scattering into the air.

"Don't shoot him!" the guy with the goatee shouted at his partner.

"Yeah, don't shoot me," I said. "It's very rude."

I swung the sword over my head and down onto the shotgun barrel. The magical blade sliced through the gun. The ruined barrel clattered to the road.

The bearded guy cried out in surprise, but he acted fast, kicking his door open and staying low as he got out of the car in case I attacked him from above. I didn't want to kill him. I had to keep these guys alive so I could find out who sent them. Although, technically, I only had to keep one of them alive for that.

I jumped down off the car and hit the back of Bearded Guy's knees with the flat part of the sword blade. He yelped and went down, rolling in the grass at the side of the road and clutching his legs.

I stood over him and cast a glance back over my shoulder, looking for Goatee Guy. He wasn't in the Taurus anymore. The driver's door was open, the seat vacant. I saw him running toward the Land Rover.

Only now he looked very different from the man who had tried to shoot out my tires. Now, he was huge, at least eight feet tall, with muscles so large that his physique would put any bodybuilder to shame. The black sweater he was wearing must be made of some type of stretchable fabric because it still clung to his enlarged body, as did his black pants.

"Shit," I said. "Ogres."

As soon as the words were out of my mouth, a roar sounded from beneath me. Bearded Guy was now also in ogre form. He swatted me away with one huge hand and I flew through the air before coming back down to earth in the grass ten feet away from where I had been standing.

"Felicity, get out of here!" I shouted. I didn't get a chance to look over at the Land Rover because Bearded Guy, now Bearded Ogre, was scrambling to his feet and getting ready to charge at me with his huge, powerful body.

He lowered his head and ran forward like a bull charging a matador.

The sword was still in my hands. I waited until the ogre was too close to change his direction and side-stepped his charge. As he stumbled past me, I sliced the broadsword through the air toward his neck. This time, I didn't use the flat of the blade.

He never knew what hit him. The enchanted blade slid through his muscles, sinews, and bones as if they were soft butter. The ogre crashed to the ground in two pieces, his head detached from his body.

I whirled around to face the Land Rover and what I saw there made my heart sink. The ogre with the goatee had one massive hand wrapped around Felicity's neck and was holding her up as if she were a rag doll. Felicity struggled against his grip, her hands clawing at his, her legs kicking in mid-air, but she had no chance against an ogre. He held her at arm's length so her kicks couldn't reach him.

He laughed when he saw the concerned look on my face. "That's right, little man, I have your woman." His voice was deep and gruff. "If you want her to live, you and I are going to take a walk in the woods together." He nodded at the weapon in my hand. "Without the sword."

I weighed my options and realized I didn't have any. The ogre was going to take me into the woods and squeeze the life out of me or he was going to kill Felicity. Maybe both.

"I want your guarantee that she won't get hurt," I said.

He chuckled. "I'm not interested in her, Harbinger, only in you."

"Before we do this," I said, "tell me who sent you to kill me. Who wants me dead so bad that they'd hire two faerie beings to do the job?"

"That is none of your concern, Investigator."

I shrugged. "If I'm about to die anyway, why not tell me who hired you?"

He shook his head. "You've made enemies in high places, that's all I'll say. Now, you drop the sword and I'll drop the woman."

I placed the sword at my feet. The blue glow playing around the blade disappeared as soon as my hand left the hilt.

"Put her down and let her drive away," I told the ogre. "Then I'll go into the woods with you."

He set Felicity down on the ground. She tried to kick his legs but he pushed her away, laughing. "I'm giving you a chance to escape," he said. "What is wrong with you, little woman?"

"Felicity," I said, "there's no point trying to kick him. Nothing short of running him over with a car is going to phase this guy."

The ogre chuckled. "Run away, little girl. What is about to happen is here is not for your eyes."

"Go, Felicity," I said. "Get in the car and drive."

She looked at me with tears in her eyes. "Alec, I can't just leave you."

"There's no choice. Get in the car."

She hesitated but then nodded. Slowly, she walked to the Land Rover and got in. The ogre came forward, still laughing at the prospect of killing me. He didn't seem too bothered that his partner was dead.

Felicity gunned the Land Rover's engine.

"Time to die, little man," the ogre growled.

"For one of us," I said.

The Land Rover shot forward, but instead of driving away, Felicity spun the steering wheel so that the vehicle came roaring over the grass toward the ogre.

The creature didn't have a chance to react. By the time he knew Felicity was trying to run him down, the Land Rover was already crashing into him. The front grille smacked squarely into his chest, knocking him down. He rolled on the grass, trying to regain his feet. But by the time he had managed to stand, the Land Rover hit him again, sending him sprawling into a thick pine tree.

I grabbed the sword from the ground. Blue flame sparked to life along the blade as I walked over to the ogre. He was dazed and probably had a few broken bones. He looked up at me as I approached. He wasn't laughing now.

"Last chance," I said. "Who sent you to kill me?"

"You can't escape your fate, Investigator," he said. "When we do not return, when it is known that you are still alive, others will come for you."

"Why is someone so interested in killing me? Who is it?"

He laughed again, but there was no mirth in it.

I swung the blade and cut off his head. Even after he was dead, his laugh drifted in the air for a couple of seconds. Felicity opened the Land Rover door, got out, dropped to her knees, and puked on the grass.

"You okay?" I asked her gently.

She got to her feet and nodded. "I'll be fine. Do we need to bury the bodies?"

"No, they're from the faerie realm, so they can't stay here for long. They'll disintegrate soon enough." I bent down and checked the ogre's pants pockets. I never knew an ogre to carry ID, but there might be something on his person that could tell me who sent him here.

The black sweater rode up his belly slightly while I was searching and I saw something on his skin. A tattoo in black ink. I pulled the sweater further up his abdomen, revealing more tattoos.

I stood back, feeling shocked.

"What is it?" Felicity asked.

"Do you recognize those tattoos?" I asked her.

She bent to examine them, her squeamishness seemingly gone. "Yeah, they're magical protection symbols."

I unbuttoned my shirt and opened it, showing her the tattoos on my own body. "Just like these."

She looked from my tattoos to those on the ogre and nodded. "Exactly the same."

"I know who hired them," I said. "They were sent here by the Society."

CHAPTER 5

THE BODIES OF THE TWO ogres began to melt into the grass. In a few seconds, their remains would be gone, leaving nothing more than a patch of earth where flowers and plants would grow faster than normal for a while. I stood watching the bodies break down, questions tumbling around inside my skull. Why was the Society trying to kill me? Why would they send faerie beings to do the job? Who had given the ogres the magical protection tattoos?

"What do you mean they're from the Society?" Felicity asked.

The bodies were gone now. "Those particular designs are tattooed on all fully-fledged investigators. They protect us from minor magic, things like location spells and some enchantments. As far as I know, only the Society of Shadows uses those exact symbols."

A car drove past us on the highway. "We should get out of here," I told Felicity. "The sight of a man standing by the side of the road holding a glowing blue sword might draw attention."

"What about their car?" she asked as we got into the Land Rover.

"We'll leave it here. It'll be stolen. Faerie beings don't own vehicles in our realm."

"When they drove up next to us, they looked like normal men," she said. "Was that a glamor?"

I nodded. "It's how faerie beings walk among us." I threw the sword onto the back seat and drove the Land Rover over the grass to the road, turning toward Leon Smith's house. Was there even a point in pursuing this case if I was on the Society's hit list? I had no idea, but right now, I had to go about my business as usual.

The day was becoming hot now, the sun climbing in a clear blue sky. I put the AC on, grateful for the chilled air as it dried the sweat on my forehead.

"Alec, it can't be the Society," Felicity said after we had driven a couple of miles. "It doesn't make sense. Why would they send you here and set up the office in Dearmont if they were just going to kill you? None of it makes sense."

"What doesn't make sense is that those ogres were tattooed with Society symbols," I told her.

She went quiet for a couple of minutes, lost in thought. Then she said, "What if it's not the Society itself but

47

someone inside the Society? Someone on the inside acting alone could have hired those ogres without the Society's knowledge."

I thought about that. It was possible. I'd pissed off enough people in the Society that a lot of them wanted me dead. And there was the fact that the ogres hadn't simply tried to shoot us—they had wanted to kill me with their bare hands in the woods, and that could be more than just their natural bloodlust. The bearded guy had tried to shoot me off the hood of the Taurus and his partner had told him not to shoot me. Maybe their job had been to make sure my death looked like the type of fate any preternatural investigator might meet: being killed by preternatural beings.

When the Society investigated my death, as they did the deaths of all investigators, they would discover that I'd been killed by ogres. There was no way they would suspect those ogres had been hired by someone in the Society, because the usual transactions between Society members and preternatural beings involved a clash of swords, the casting of curses, and, ultimately, death for one or both parties.

Was it possible that a Society member had formed a temporary truce with the preternatural world just to kill me and cover his tracks? Or her tracks, of course. There were plenty of women in the Society who would like to see me ripped apart by ogres.

"You could be right," I told Felicity. "Let's say someone in the Society wants me dead. They make a deal with the ogres, hire them as hitmen. As part of the deal, they give the ogres the protection tattoos. They hide the wearer from location spells and protect them from minor magic. For an ogre living in the faerie realm, that could be useful. And it benefits the Society guy because the tattoos protect the would-be assassins from me."

She frowned in confusion. "You don't use magic, Alec." Then her eyes widened. "Do you?"

"Before you tell me which regulation in the Investigative Guidebook that breaks, no, I don't. But I've employed witches in the past to help me."

"Really? Because that breaks a whole chapter of rules in the guidebook."

"Nothing is as black and white as the guidebook makes it out to be," I said. The GPS directed us off the highway and along a narrow road that wound through the woods before the female voice said, "You have reached your destination on the right."

On the right, a short road led to a large iron gate set into a high stone wall. I drove up to it. There was an intercom system on the wall, a small metal box with a talk button and built-in speaker. A camera pointed down at us from atop the gate.

Leaving the engine running, I got out and walked to the intercom.

After I pressed the button, a young male voice answered. "Who is it?"

"My name is Alec Harbinger," I said. "My assistant, Felicity Lake, called you earlier. We'd like to talk to you about Dark Rock Lake."

"Sure, come on up." There was a buzz and the gate swung open slowly.

I got back in the Land Rover and drove inside, whistling with appreciation at the expansive grounds beyond the wall. A huge, well-maintained lawn stretched from the walls all the way to a huge mansion that sat proudly in the center of the grounds. The house was all modern angles and glass walls. I preferred old buildings, myself, but even so, I could appreciate the design of this modern-day palace.

"Someone has some serious money," Felicity said. "This place is as big as a golf course."

The road we were on was paved with white gravel which formed a circle by the front door of the house. Parked in that circle were a number of expensive cars, including Rolls Royces and Bentleys.

I parked my old Land Rover between a metallic-blue Ferrari Spider and a silver Bentley and climbed out. Felicity followed me to the front door, fishing her notebook and pen out of her purse.

The door was opened by a young black guy wearing a gray hoodie and blue jeans. I guessed his age to be early twenties, probably a couple of years older than his friend, James Robinson. "Hey," he said. "Come in."

"Leon Smith?" I asked as we stepped into a marble-floored hallway. The glass ceiling took advantage of the natural light, making the house bright and airy.

"Yeah, that's me," he said. "Come on, I'll get Michael to make us some drinks. Iced tea?"

"Sure, thanks," I said, and Felicity nodded.

A tall, white man in his sixties appeared from a side door and spoke to Leon with a British accent. "I'm sorry I didn't get the door, sir, I was occupied with the arrangements regarding the party on Friday."

"Leave that for now, Michael. I'd like iced tea for my guests and me out back."

"Of course, sir. Then I will immediately return to the matter of the party."

Leon sighed. "Sure, whatever." He led us through the house and outside to an area paved with flagstones and surrounded by a low, ornate stone wall. There was a long, low table out here along with outdoor furniture that probably cost more than my house.

"Please, sit," Leon said, "and I'll answer whatever questions I can."

We sat and Felicity asked him, "Do you mind if I take notes?"

Leon shook his head. "Of course not."

"You seem very open to us being here," I told him. "If I was approached by detectives wanting to ask me questions, I'd be a little guarded."

"I've been expecting someone to come here," he said. "In fact, I'm surprised you didn't show up sooner. You were hired by James's parents, right?"

I nodded. "Why were you expecting someone to come here?"

Michael appeared with a pitcher of iced tea and three tall glasses. He poured the drinks and left.

After the butler had left, Leon said, "That weekend was weird, man. James and Sarah changed, and I mean really changed. James is my best friend, but I haven't seen him since we went to the lake. I knew his parents would try and find out what happened that weekend. I would if my son returned home totally changed. James is supposed to be my best friend, but he and Sarah didn't even come back with us. They came home a day later."

"Who's Sarah?" I asked.

"Sarah Silverman. She was James's girlfriend. Well, she was his girlfriend for that weekend. James changes his women as often as I change my socks. But I think things were a bit more serious with Sarah. The Silverman family live next door to James's family, just on the other side of the woods between their houses, so they've known each other for a long time, but this was the first time I knew about her being his girlfriend. It was a surprise to me."

"Okay," I said. "Who else went to the lake that weekend?"

"There were seven of us. James, me, Sarah, Ed Kowalski, Alicia Jones—she's Ed's girlfriend—Mike Halliwell, and Scott Peterson."

Felicity wrote down the names.

I took a sip of iced tea. It chilled my mouth and throat, but that was a welcome sensation in the heat of the day. "Tell me about the party," I said.

Leon shrugged. "It was the type of party you'd expect a group of rich kids to have. We drove up to the lake on Friday night. We had a truck full of beer, liquor, and food. It was cold that night, but we had a barbecue on the beach. There was a lot of drinking and music. We had a good time. We rented three cabins. There's a dozen cabins by the lake, but the others were empty that weekend, so we had the whole place to ourselves."

"Three cabins between seven people," Felicity said. "What were the sleeping arrangements?"

"I shared with Mike and Scott. James and Sarah had a cabin to themselves and so did Ed and Alicia. James and Ed still live with their parents so they were using the getaway for a weekend of wild sex, you know?"

"I do know," Felicity said enigmatically.

That seemed to take Leon by surprise. He paused a moment before continuing. "So, yeah, that was the Friday. Everything was great. No weirdness, nothing out of the ordinary. On Saturday, I got up around noon and told myself I was never going to drink again. I had a hangover like you wouldn't believe."

"Were there drugs at this party?" I asked.

"Yeah, but I don't get involved with those."

"Did James and Sarah?"

"Yeah, I guess. I don't remember if they did anything that weekend, but it's possible."

"Tell me when things started to turn weird," I said.

"That was Saturday night. The day was mostly quiet because everyone was hung over. When it started to get dark, Scott built a fire on the beach and that got most people back into the party mood. Someone fired up the barbecue and the drinks began to flow. It was more subdued than the night before, but most of us got drunk again."

"What about James and his girlfriend? Did they get drunk, too?"

"Yeah, they did. We were all sitting around the fire at midnight and they kept saying they were going to go for a walk in the woods, but I think they were a little scared because Ed had been telling ghost stories earlier. So James and Sarah were kind of daring each other to be the first to get up and go into the trees."

"What was the night like?" I asked. "Was there a full moon?"

Leon shook his head. "I don't think so. It was a dark night. I don't remember seeing any moon at all."

"A new moon, maybe," I said.

"What does that have to do with anything, man?" Leon asked.

"Maybe nothing," I said. I'd forgotten that Leon thought we were mundane detectives. "I'm just trying to form a mental image of that night."

"It was dark," he said. "And cold. We were huddled around the fire, and to tell the truth, I was looking forward to getting into bed. But James and Sarah kept daring each other to go into the woods. Eventually, James stood up and held out his hand to Sarah. She took it and they both went off into the trees."

"Okay," I said. "And what happened next?"

Leon shrugged. "Nothing. At least not for a while. We waited, expecting them to come back to the fire after a few minutes, but they didn't. After a while, we began calling them, but there was no answer. We assumed they were getting it on in the woods, you know?"

I nodded. "So when did they come back?"

"Well, like I said, we called and there was no answer so eventually, we went to our cabins and went to bed."

"You just left them out there?" Felicity asked, looking up from her notebook.

"We felt like idiots waiting there and freezing our asses off. So, yeah, we went to bed. James and Sarah were both adults and we weren't responsible for them. We thought they were just having some fun together."

"When did you see them again?" I asked.

"I didn't see them until the next morning. But I heard them return to their cabin later that night. I didn't sleep so well because Mike was snoring. When James and Sarah came back, I was in the kitchen of our cabin, drinking coffee."

"What time was that?" Felicity asked.

"Around 3 a.m."

"You say you heard them but didn't see them," I said. "How do you know it was James and Sarah? You could have heard someone from one of the other cabins and assumed it was James and Sarah returning."

He shrugged. "Yeah, maybe." He drank some of his iced tea and then added, "But I'm pretty sure it was them. I think I heard James laugh when they opened the door to their cabin."

"Did you hear anything else?"

He paused and took another drink. "I did hear something else. When they came out of the woods and walked across the beach, I'm sure they were dragging something on the ground."

"Something heavy?" I asked.

"I have no idea, man. At the time, I thought they were dragging a tree branch or something, maybe something to play a prank on us because we'd gone to bed while they were still out there. But the next day. I realized that wasn't it." He leaned forward and lowered his voice. "They found something in the woods and brought it back with them, but it wasn't any tree branch."

I leaned toward him and lowered my own voice to match his. "What was it?"

"I don't know. But whatever it was, they didn't want the rest of us to see it. The next day, they were both acting really weird and when Ed said he was going to go into their cabin to look for more beer, both James and Sarah totally flipped out. Ed was at their cabin door and James tackled him to the ground and started beating on him. We had to drag him off Ed, otherwise I think he would have killed him."

"And you have no idea what they were hiding in the cabin?"

Leon shook his head. "No, they wouldn't let us anywhere near the cabin after that. Both of them sat by the door, like they were guarding whatever was inside."

"Were they acting weird before that?" Felicity asked.

"Yeah, they were," Leon said. "It was like they didn't want to speak to us at all. At first we thought that maybe they were pissed because we went to bed while they were still in the woods. But it was more than that. I've known James since we were kids, so I can usually tell what sort of mood he's in. That day, he wasn't just pissed. The way he looked at us, the way he looked at me, it was like there was a malevolence in his gaze. If looks could kill, the police would have found our bodies on that beach, you know?"

I said, "Was there anything strange about his eyes?"

He frowned. "In what way?"

"Did they glow or change color? Anything like that?"

"Err … no." He looked at me suspiciously, then at Felicity. "You guys are just normal detectives, right?"

Felicity decided to use that moment to pick up her glass and take a big drink of iced tea, avoiding the question.

I sighed and looked at the remaining iced tea in my own glass, wondering if I'd have time to drink it before we got kicked out of here. I've been kicked out of a lot of places after revealing the true nature of my job.

"What do you mean by normal detectives?" I asked Leon.

"The kind of private eyes that trace missing people and trail dudes having affairs."

"No," I said, "we're not that kind of detective."

His eyes widened slightly and he looked from Felicity to me. "Are you those preternatural guys?"

"We're preternatural investigators, yes," I said. I picked up my glass and drained the contents.

"Awesome," Leon said. "I've seen those P.I. offices before but I've never met an actual investigator. Do you think what happened to James is, like, demon possession or something?"

"We don't know," I said. "That's why we're investigating the case."

"Yeah, but for you guys to get involved, there has to be some kind of supernatural involvement, right?"

"Yes, but in this case, we're not sure if there is any. That's what we're trying to ascertain."

He nodded in understanding. "What do you think now that you've spoken to me?"

"I'd like to know what James and Sarah found in those woods."

"We all would," he said. "Whatever that thing was, it made them go crazy."

"What else did they do that was strange?" I poured more iced tea from the pitcher into my glass and offered some to Felicity and Leon. They both accepted. The ice clinked into their glasses as I poured.

"Like I said, they stared at us like we were their worst enemies. And they barely spoke except to each other, and even then, it was in whispers. They were creepy, man. When we said we were ready to head home, they said they were staying at the lake for another night. They'd driven up there together in James's Bronco with Mike in the back so Mike had to come back to Dearmont with me in my Jag. Believe me, he was more than happy about that. He didn't want to be in a truck with those two."

"If you had to describe the James and Sarah that came out of those woods in one word," I said, "what would it be?"

"Creepy," Leon said without hesitation.

"And you haven't seen either of them since?"

"No, and that's strange in itself. Even when I was busy working, James would come over to the house on weekends and just hang out. But since that weekend at the lake, he hasn't even called me." He thought for a moment and then added, "Not that I'd want him to. I spoke to his mother a couple of weeks ago and she said he's been taking nightly walks in the woods around their house. She knew there was something very wrong and asked me about that weekend."

"What did you tell her?"

"The same thing I just told you. She didn't seem to believe that I didn't know about what had happened to James. That's why I thought she'd hire a private detective. But she hired you guys instead. There must be a reason why she did that."

I shrugged. "Her son's personality and behavior changed over the course of a single weekend. Some parents might attribute that to the supernatural because it's easier to believe that a demon has possessed your son than face the fact that he may have mental health issues brought on by drugs or alcohol abuse."

"You think James has mental issues?" he asked.

"It's something I'd be wondering, except for the fact that Sarah was affected in exactly the same way at exactly the same time."

"So it could be a demon?" He seemed genuinely excited by that idea.

"Like I said, we don't know. But thanks for talking to us, you've been a great help." I drank the last of my iced tea and got up. Felicity did likewise.

"No problem," Leon said, also getting to his feet. "You know, if you guys ever need any computer work done, give me a call."

"You work in computers?" Felicity asked him.

"Yeah, I write code, design apps and games, that kind of thing. It pays for all of this." He indicated the house and grounds. As he led us back through the house, he grabbed a business card from a stack on a marble table and handed it to Felicity.

I thanked him again for his help and we left the house, walking across the gravel to the Land Rover.

"What do you think?" Felicity asked me.

"I think I'm in the wrong line of work."

"Money can't buy everything." She climbed into the Land Rover.

"No," I said as I slid into the driver's seat and started the engine. "But it bought all these cars."

She raised an eyebrow. "I thought you loved this old Land Rover."

"I do, but that doesn't mean I wouldn't like a Ferrari, too."

"Anyway, when I asked you what you thought, I meant about what Leon told us. Do you still think this is The Case of the Moody Teenager?"

"No, I don't," I said as I backed out from between the Ferrari and the Bentley. I pointed the Land Rover in the direction of the gate. "I think this is The Case of Something Weird Happened at the Lake."

CHAPTER 6

WE DROVE IN SILENCE FOR a while. The only sound was the constant rumble of the engine and the woman's voice from the GPS, directing us to Amelia Robinson's house. Felicity had programmed in the new destination and then sat back, watching the tall trees roll past the window. I assumed she was lost in her own thoughts in the case. I tried to focus on the case, myself, but my thoughts kept returning to one burning question.

Who was trying to kill me?

I knew there were some members if the Inner Circle who wanted me to be thrown out of the Society of Shadows after the events in Paris, but would any of them go as far as hiring preternatural assassins? It seemed like overkill.

"Alec," Felicity said, "what happened in Paris?"

Maybe she had been thinking about the attempted assassination, too. I guess that made sense; she could have been killed.

"I'll tell you later," I said.

"Later today?"

"Yeah, sure. I was planning on having a barbecue later in my yard. Why don't you join me and I'll tell you everything? I guess you have a right to know since you got dragged into the attempt on my life."

She nodded. "Sounds good. I'll bring the beer."

"Deal. You know my address?"

"Of course."

Yeah, of course she did. My father would make sure she was able to keep an eye on me outside of work hours. The Society had probably set her up in a house close to mine. Maybe even on the same street.

"So, where do you live?" I asked her, trying to sound casual.

Felicity grinned. "I'm your next door neighbor, Alec."

"Of course you are," I said. "Well, at least you won't have far to come for the barbecue." I wasn't sure what I thought of having my assistant living next door. I liked to keep some distance between my personal life and my work life. When I went home from work, at whatever time that might be, I wanted to relax, chill out, and try to forget about work. With Felicity living so close, that might not be possible.

"Don't worry," Felicity said, as if reading my mind. "I keep myself to myself and I don't talk shop outside of office hours."

"Cool," I said noncommittally.

The GPS guided us off the highway and along a road that led us to another wall and gate. Unlike Leon Smith's gate, this one was made of wrought iron fashioned into a decorative, curved pattern, and beyond it, I could see the driveway leading up to the Robinson house.

There was no locking mechanism on the gate, so I opened it and drove up to the house. Where Leon Smith's house had been modern, the Robinson place looked like it might have been built in the nineteenth century and had sections added at later dates. It was traditional in design and seemed to sprawl across the landscape. The grounds around the house were heavily-wooded apart from a front lawn that reached down to an area where a large pond sat beneath a willow tree.

I parked the Land Rover near the house and got out. The air held a sharp tang of pine from the woods.

The front door opened and Amelia Robinson came out to greet us. She was still wearing the elegant clothes she had worn in the office earlier, but now she had added a pair of sunglasses to her ensemble.

"Thank you for coming," she said. "James hasn't emerged from his room. Would you like to go up and knock on his door?"

"Before we do that," I said, "can you show me where he goes at night?"

"Of course." She pointed to a section of the woods around the side of the house. "That's where he disappears into the trees. I have no idea where he goes after that."

"We'll go check that out first," I said. "Does James's bedroom window overlook that part of the woods?"

Amelia glanced toward the house and nodded. "Yes, it does."

I opened up the back of the Land Rover. "If you could just go about your business as usual, Amelia, that would be great. I'm pretty sure James will be coming out of his room shortly."

"All right," she said, sounding a little confused. "I'll go back inside."

"That would be great," I repeated.

She went in through the front door and closed it.

I reached into the back of the Land Rover and pulled aside the heavy canvas blanket that covered my equipment. The tools of my trade lay neatly in the trunk. Since I never knew what I was going to be up against, I had everything in here from shovels to dig up coffins, to ouija boards to contact lost spirits, to pieces of white chalk for drawing emergency wards and sigils. There was a vampire hunter's kit from Victorian London, plastic bags of salt, and a number of herbal concoctions in various glass jars. There were also a couple of daggers in leather sheaths, a crowbar, and a shotgun. The shotgun shells had silver shot mixed in with the normal steel.

I took a dagger and fixed it to my belt, just in case. At least Felicity would be satisfied that I was now armed. I pulled the bottom of my shirt over the sheathed dagger, hiding it.

Then I grabbed a shovel, covered over the rest of the equipment with the canvas, and closed the trunk.

"Are we digging for something?" Felicity asked, eyeing the shovel in my hand.

"That's what we want James to think," I said. "Come on, let's go for a walk."

We sauntered across the sunny lawn, taking our time to get to the edge of the dark woods.

"Do you think he saw us?" Felicity whispered, looking over at the house.

"Yeah, I'm certain of it. Whatever he and Sarah found at Dark Rock Lake, they probably hid it somewhere in the woods. That's why James comes in here every night. He's visiting it for some reason. Whatever it is, it's important to him, so he's going to be keeping an eye out in case anyone discovers what he's hiding."

I made a dramatic pointing gesture toward the trees and said loudly, "It's in there." Even if James wasn't watching the window at that particular moment, hearing my voice should get his attention.

"Let's go dig it up," Felicity almost shouted.

I thought I saw some curtains move at one of the upper level windows but I couldn't be sure.

"If it's in there, we'll find it," I said loud enough to be heard a mile away. I stepped out of the sunlight and into the shadows beneath the trees and immediately felt cooler. The air smelled strongly of pine and earth and rotting wood. I could hear squirrels in the trees somewhere close by and birds singing in the high branches above.

"This place is creepy," Felicity whispered.

"If we couldn't hear the birds and squirrels, then it would be creepy," I said. "Animals have an innate sense for the supernatural and usually avoid places where there's a strong evil presence."

I looked back across the sunlit lawn to the house. No sign of James. "Let's go farther in," I said. "We might discover what it is that James finds so interesting here."

After making our way over fallen branches and roots that rose from the earth like thick tentacles, we found a dirt trail leading deeper into the woods. "This looks like it's been here a long time," I said, inspecting the hard-packed dirt. "I wonder where it leads."

"Only one way to find out," Felicity said. Following the trail was better than wandering aimlessly in the woods and possibly getting lost, so we followed the well-trodden path. The trail was only wide enough for one person, so I took the lead with Felicity close behind.

"Keep an eye out for anything strange," I said.

"Like what?"

"I have no idea."

The woods were gloomy and mysterious even though it was midday. I wondered what this place would be like during the night time. Probably ten times creepier than it was now.

"I see something ahead," I said. There was a building there, through the trees, I was sure of it. I increased my pace and Felicity did the same to keep up with me.

The trail led to a wide clearing. The clearing was ringed with a low wrought-iron fence that matched the front gate we had driven through earlier. Within the fence, a number of gravestones stood among overgrown grass and brambles. The center piece of the graveyard was a tall stone mausoleum; the structure I had seen back on the trail. It was adorned with weeping stone angels and the name ROBINSON was engraved above the door.

"I think we found where James comes at night," I said.

Felicity shivered. "Now that's creepy."

CHAPTER 7

A SMALL IRON GATE IN the fence was unlocked. I opened it and stepped through. Felicity went to the nearest gravestone and read the worn words on its surface.

"This has been here since 1899," she said. "A man named Luke Robinson is buried here. He was 32 when he died."

"So this is the family burial ground." The stone closest to me belonged to a Flora Robinson who died in 1934.

"So, what is it that James finds interesting here?" she asked.

Using the shovel, I began to pull the long grass and brambles aside. "Search the ground. Maybe he buried it here somewhere."

She swept her hand through the grass and then yelled, "Ow, that hurt!" Stepping back, she held up her thumb so I could see the trickle of bright blood running from it.

"Watch out for the thorns," I said.

"Now you tell me." She continued her search, but more carefully this time, pulling at the overgrown grass tentatively.

I crouched down and took a closer look at the thorny branches near my feet. The branches were flowering, the little flowers white with pink-tipped stamen. I recognized it as hawthorn. Standing up again, I used the shovel to push the branches aside so I could inspect the earth beneath.

We searched the area for a couple of minutes before we heard a shout from the trail. "Hey, you! What are you doing?"

I turned to see a young, fair-haired man striding toward us. He was dressed in a black T-shirt, blue jeans, and boots. I wondered how fast he had thrown the clothing on after seeing us from his window.

I gave him a quick smile. "James Robinson, I presume?"

"Yeah, I'm James Robinson," he said, coming through the open gate. "Who the hell are you and why are you in my family's graveyard?"

Now that he was closer to me, I inspected his face, especially his eyes. I always went by the old adage that the eyes are the windows to the soul. In the case of demon possession, they were the first place you looked for something out of the ordinary, usually flecks of red in the iris.

I couldn't see anything strange in James's eyes. They were blue with a little gray, but definitely no red.

"My name is Alec Harbinger," I said, extending my hand, "and this is my assistant, Felicity Lake."

He didn't shake my hand. Instead, he pointed at me with his own, his forefinger jabbing at the air between us. "What the hell are you doing here? Why are you in these woods?"

"We're just looking around," I said enigmatically.

"With a shovel?"

"That just helps me look deeper."

His eyes might have been totally normal-looking, but they burned with fury. "You are going to get out of here right now or I'm going to call security."

"Go ahead," I said. "We're here at your mother's invitation."

"Oh, is that right? And does she know you're digging up our graveyard?"

I couldn't really answer that, so I just shrugged.

"What is going on here?" came a voice from the trail. Amelia Robinson appeared, tottering unsteadily on her high heels. She made it to the fence and stayed there, leaning on it. "Mr. Harbinger, what are you doing? I told you that discretion was of utmost importance."

"He's digging up our ancestors," James said. "He said he's here at your invitation. What's going on, Mother?"

She hesitated, looking from her son to me to the shovel in my hand. Finally, she said, "I asked Mr. Harbinger to come here and speak with you about what happened at the lake that weekend. You haven't been the same since you returned, James. I'm just worried about you."

The fury in his eyes increased. "You hired a detective to question me? I don't believe this. You're treating your own son like a criminal."

"I ... I'm sorry, James, but I didn't know what else to do."

"I'll tell you what you can do," he said, pointing at her the same way he had pointed at me. "You can leave me alone." Then he whirled on me. "And you can take your secretary and get off our property."

"That isn't your decision to make," I said. "Your mother hired me."

Amelia looked at me and said, "You should go. I don't require your services anymore."

I sighed. "Amelia, if it's because of what happened here, I can assure you that...."

"Go," she said, her voice firm.

James chuckled. "I guess you're off the case, Detective."

I ignored him and stepped through the open gate. I wasn't sure why I felt disappointed; the case was a bust anyway. I hadn't found any evidence of preternatural activity and I had lost my first client in Maine. Case closed.

"Don't forget to take your secretary," James said, his voice light and airy now that he knew we were leaving.

Felicity was already walking past him toward the open gate. James grinned and swatted her butt.

Felicity moved with the speed of a tigress, pivoting on one foot and facing James before using both hands to push against his chest. He stumbled backward toward the iron fence, lost his footing and fell. He tried to stop his fall with his left hand, but as soon as it touched the fence, he withdrew it just like Felicity had withdrawn her hand from the hawthorn.

But James's hand wasn't bleeding, it was smoking.

A burn mark crossed his palm where the iron had touched it. He bent over and cradled his hand, pain etched across his face. Looking at Felicity over his shoulder, he yelled, "You stupid bitch, you'll pay for that!"

Calmly, Felicity walked through the open gate and joined me on the path, whispering, "That was interesting."

"It certainly was," I whispered to her. Raising my voice to a normal level, I said, "Amelia, if you still want us to take this case…."

"No, Mr. Harbinger, I don't. Coming to see you was a mistake. Please leave before I decide to sue your assistant for assault."

Felicity made a move toward the older woman. I grabbed her arm before she unleashed a right hook. "Come on," I said. "We're done here."

She nodded and turned to face me. "Let's go."

We walked back along the path, leaving Amelia and James at the graveyard. When we emerged from the shadows of the trees into the sunlight, I blinked at the sudden brightness, a welcome change after being in those gloomy woods. As we walked across the lawn, I relished the warmth of the sun on my face. But by the time we reached the Land Rover, I was too hot, and ready to crank up the AC.

I got in and started the engine, closing my eyes as cold air blasted from the vents against my face. "You saw what happened back there, right?" Felicity asked.

"You mean when you kicked his ass? Hell yeah, way to go."

She rolled her eyes. "No, I mean when he touched that iron fence."

I grinned. "Oh, yeah, I saw that."

"That isn't James Robinson back there," she said. "That's a faerie."

"Exactly what I was thinking." I drove down the driveway toward the gate.

Felicity asked, "But if there's a faerie assuming the likeness of James Robinson and pretending to be him, then where is the real James?"

"That's where it gets complicated," I said. "The real James Robinson is trapped in the faerie realm."

CHAPTER 8

$\mathbf{A}$S WE DROVE BACK TO Dearmont, a pang of hunger growled in my stomach. I hadn't eaten anything since the apple bakes this morning and it was now past lunch time. "Shall we grab a bite to eat while we talk about what we're going to do next?" I asked Felicity.

"Sounds good. There's a diner on this side of town that makes excellent burgers. Darla's Diner. Just follow the highway back toward Dearmont. We passed the diner on the way out here."

"Did we? I don't remember a diner," I said. I usually made a mental note of every eating establishment I passed, especially those close to home. The nature of my work meant I didn't always have time to cook a meal, so restaurants and diners were a valuable resource.

"We were being chased by ogres at the time," she reminded me.

"Ah, that explains it."

Up ahead on the highway, I saw the dark green Taurus the ogres had been driving. It attached to a tow truck. Parked behind the tow truck was a black and white police cruiser, and standing watching the proceedings was the big sheriff I had seen on the internet, John Cantrell. He stood with his hands on his hips, watching the car with the busted hood and engine as its front end was lifted into the air by the crane on the back of the truck.

When I'd seen Sheriff John Cantrell in the picture, standing by the lake, I had thought that he might wrestle grizzlies in his free time. Now that I saw him in real life, I figured bears would be too easy an opponent for this huge man. A T-rex might be more worthy an adversary.

As we drove past, I looked for the redhead deputy, but she was nowhere to be seen.

Darla's Diner was a mile farther along the highway, a long, low building with a frontage that was mainly chrome and glass, glinting in the sun. A dozen trucks and cars waited in the parking lot and through the windows, I could see diners sitting at the tables, eating.

"This a pretty busy place," I said to Felicity.

"I told you, they make good burgers." She waited for me to park before jumping out and heading for the door. I followed, wondering if we'd get a table or have to eat in the car. I didn't mind either way; I'd eaten in the Land

Rover plenty of times. There was a collection of takeout boxes and containers in the back seat that could attest to that.

The interior of Darla's was furnished just like a million other diners in the country: counter and stools running almost half the length of the place, tables here and there, and booths by the windows with red vinyl upholstery.

As I followed Felicity through the glass door into the air-conditioned establishment, the mouth-watering smell of fried meat and onions hit me, making my stomach rumble. The diner was noisy with sound of chattering customers and country music drifting from speakers mounted in the walls. That was good. It meant I could talk to Felicity without being overheard. In a quieter place, we would have to lower our voices so that we couldn't be heard by eavesdropping customers or staff.

Felicity found a booth and slipped into it. I caught the eye of a waitress who was serving coffee to a group of truckers at the counter and took a seat across the table from Felicity.

The waitress, a woman in her late-forties with curly blonde hair pinned up on her head, came over with a pen poised over her order pad. Her name, Sandra, was embroidered on the left breast of her uniform. She smiled at us. "Hi, and welcome to Darla's. Have you eaten with us before?"

"I have," Felicity said, "but my friend hasn't."

Sandra turned her attention to me. "We have menus here," she said, pointing to the menus in a chrome holder on the table, "and specials on the board. If there's anything particular you'd like us to cook for you, or if you have any dietary requirements, you just let me know."

"Whatever that burger is that I can smell," I said. "I want that."

She grinned. "We have a selection of burgers listed on the menu right here." She took one of the menus and opened it in front of me, pointing out the list of burgers.

"Whichever is the biggest," I said.

Sandra nodded. "That would be the Darla's Double Burger. It's two meat patties inside a sesame bun and it comes with tomatoes, onions, lettuce, dill pickle, and mayonnaise. Do you want cheese on that?"

"Everything," I said.

"Fries?"

"Definitely."

Felicity ordered a cheese burger and we both ordered sodas. Sandra asked us if we wanted coffee and filled our cups from a pot when we both said yes. After she had gone, I said to Felicity, "Good choice. This is great. If the food is as good as it smells, this could be our regular lunch place."

Felicity laughed. "If you have a Darla's Double Burger for lunch every day, you won't be able to catch any bad guys."

"I'll be fine. I work out with a heavy bag and weights every day. And I do weapons training most days, too. That burns off a lot of calories. Of course, I need to find my bag and unpack it, but once I do, I'll get back to the workouts."

"Your punch bag is in your basement," she said. "Along with your training weapons and weights. I oversaw the arrival of all your stuff and I made sure everything went to the correct rooms."

"I have a basement?"

A smile flickered across her lips. "You really need to get acquainted with your new home. There's a large basement area that the previous owners used as a gym. I assumed you'd want to use it for the same purpose, even if your equipment is a little more exotic than theirs was. You should have seen the looks on the faces of the men from the removal company when they were bringing the training swords and throwing daggers into the house, not to mention the training dummies that have obviously been stabbed repeatedly by those daggers."

"All of that stuff should have been in boxes," I said. "Trust the Society to screw it up."

"It was boxed up, but one of the blades must have cut through the cardboard and the weapons went spilling out over the lawn. Like I said, you should have seen the looks on the removal men's faces." She smiled at the memory. She had a pretty smile. In fact, Felicity had a pretty everything, but I was trying not to notice. My life was complicated enough without noticing how attractive my assistant was. None of my past relationships had ended well. At the time, I had blamed that on nature of my job, but lately I had come to realize that I had a self-destructive nature where intimacy was concerned. I never let any woman get too close to me, and when a relationship inevitably headed that way, I ended it.

In fact, the only thing I had that was anything like a relationship at the moment was with my friend, Mallory Bronson, and our time together could hardly be called intimate. I wondered if Mallory would show up in Dearmont soon. She had my new address. It would be good to see a familiar face in these unfamiliar parts.

"I think I managed to get all your boxes into the correct rooms," Felicity said, her voice cutting into my thoughts.

"Well, thanks for sorting everything out," I said. Felicity was right; I needed to unpack all my stuff. I was here to stay, whether I liked it or not, so I might as well get used to the idea.

Sandra returned with our drinks and burgers. My mouth watered so much when I saw the burger and fries on the plate in front of me that I wondered if the cook might be casting a faerie glamor over the food. No burger had the right to look so juicy and tempting.

When I took a mouthful, the tender meat, crispy onions, and fresh garnishing created a taste sensation in my mouth that made me close my eyes and go, "Mmmm."

A grin crossed Felicity's face. "I knew you'd like it."

Swallowing the little piece of heaven that was a Darla's Double Burger, I said, "This is definitely our lunch place. Now, we need to discuss our next move in the James Robinson case."

"We're off the case," Felicity reminded me. "Mrs. Robinson fired us."

"Yes, she did. So refund her money. We're going to have to log this as a Society Case. It means we'll get paid peanuts for solving it, but we don't have a choice." It was every investigator's intention to find and hold on to private clients. It was how we became aware of preternatural activity in the area we worked. The best case scenario was to solve the case and get paid by the client because the private rates were good. But if the client got cold feet for whatever reason and fired us, we had a duty to carry out every job to its conclusion once we had established a preternatural presence.

The Society of Shadows had been fighting the supernatural since its formation in London, England, in the year 1682. It didn't care how much investigators got paid and only used the private cases to root out preternatural beings. If we couldn't keep a client for whatever reason, the case became a Society Case, which meant the Society paid us to solve it at a flat daily rate. If we didn't get clients coming through our doors, we were expected to scour local news reports to find possible preternatural activity and bill the Society at those low rates.

The loss of Mrs. Robinson as a client meant I was basically working her case for free, but I had to see it to the end. Otherwise, I'd be breaking the Society's rules, and that never ended well.

"Okay, I'll put it in the books as a Society Case," Felicity said. "We've definitely established a preternatural presence."

"Yeah, you saw how that creature reacted when it touched iron. It's a faerie being."

"The question is, why is it pretending to be James Robinson?" She took a drink of her soda and waited for me to provide the answer to that question.

"No," I said. "The question is, where is the real James Robinson? We don't need to know the faerie's motive. Faeries like to play tricks and games. It probably took on James's identity simply because it could."

"Do you think James and Sarah are dead?"

"No, they're not dead. They'll be trapped in Faerie. Somewhere in the woods by Dark Rock Lake there will be a place where the barrier between our world and Faerie is unstable. Those places are usually marked by hawthorn bushes. Hawthorn is strongly connected with the faerie realm. If we find a hawthorn bush in the woods, that's where James and Sarah will have been lured into Faerie."

Her voice dropped to a whisper despite the fact that nobody could hear her anyway in the noisy diner. "Can you bring them back?"

I nodded. "It means travelling to Faerie to get them, but I can do it."

"What would happen then? There'd be two James Robinsons and two Sarah Silvermans."

"We'd take them to their homes and confront the faerie beings. Remember, the faeries aren't really James or Sarah, they only look like them because of a glamor. Once the real James and Sarah show up, the glamor will be broken, and we'll see those creatures for what they really are."

"And then?"

"And then I kill them."

She nodded and took a bite of her burger.

There was no other acceptable outcome to this. These faeries had meddled in human affairs, so they had to die. It was because of events like this that the Society of Shadows existed; to protect humans from preternatural beings.

"So, when do we go to Dark Rock Lake?" Felicity asked.

"Tomorrow," I said. "It's too late to drive up there today. We'd be stumbling around in the dark by the time we got there. I need to take some equipment, too, and that's in a box somewhere at my house, so I have to find it before we leave."

"Check the boxes in the room next to the master bedroom."

Well, that would make things much easier. My stuff might be still packed into boxes, but it seemed that Felicity had categorized the boxes to make my life easier. "I will. Thanks."

We ate in silence for a while and I concentrated on the way the burger tantalized my taste buds. From the speakers on the walls, Kenny Rogers was singing about a gambler. Through the window, I watched the cars traveling up and down the highway, the sun glinting off their windshields.

"What's the plan for the rest of the day?" Felicity asked me as she finished her burger.

"I guess we return to the office, check the answering machine, and hang around there for a while. If it looks like we aren't going to get any new clients, we can go home." Now that we had lost Mrs. Robinson and were only going to make the Society flat rate of pay on her case, we needed more clients if we were going to survive.

I waved at Sandra and got the check, leaving her a substantial tip even though I could barely afford it at the moment. But that burger had been so good. Anyway, I could bill the lunch to the Society now that they were picking up the tab for this case.

Outside, the day had heated up even more. I was definitely having a barbecue in the yard later, and a couple of cold beers. I saw the black and white police cruiser pull off the highway and enter the parking lot just as I was getting into the Land Rover. Sheriff Cantrell was behind the wheel. I started the engine and backed away from the diner as the big man heaved his bulk out of the patrol car and went inside.

He would be investigating what had happened to the stolen Taurus, particularly how the hood and engine had been cut by some sort of blade. He'd probably still be wondering about that after he retired because I was pretty sure that "enchanted sword" was outside his list of possibilities, and there would be no sign of the car thieves now that they'd been reduced to faerie remains.

I joined the traffic on the highway and drove toward Dearmont at a sedate speed.

When we reached Main Street, I said to Felicity, "Looks like we have a client." Standing outside the door to our building was a tall young man in a T-shirt and black jeans, wearing thick-rimmed glasses on his hawkish face. He cast nervous glances up and down the street while he waited and checked his watch constantly. "I'll drop you here," I told Felicity as we reached the corner before our block. "You take the guy inside and find out what he wants while I park around back."

She nodded and I let her out of the Land Rover. While she crossed the street toward the nervous-looking young man, I drove around the back of the building and left the Land Rover in the same space it had occupied earlier. While I was walking away from the parking space and busy checking my cell for messages or texts, I bumped into someone on the sidewalk. When I looked up from the phone to apologize, I was momentarily startled.

The woman was in her late twenties and pretty in a dark-eyed, dark-haired, sultry kind of way. She wore a dress of lace and black velvet that was probably modelled on something out of the Victorian era, and she carried a parasol that was made of black lace, fashioned into intricate, delicate patterns.

But it wasn't her beauty or anachronistic dress sense that startled me; as my gaze met hers, I knew I was looking into the eyes of a witch.

When you've worked with the preternatural world for as long as I have, you tend to recognize other human beings who have had the same experiences. It's like if two bodybuilders met at a party, they would instantly understand that they shared a common interest. In their case, of course, the huge muscles would be a dead giveaway. In the case of people who have experienced the other realms or magic, things that most human beings didn't believe were real, the recognition was more subtle. It was at a subconscious level but it was there all the same.

So I knew that this woman was no stranger to magic and, judging by her dress, I concluded that she was a witch. At the same time, she knew that I was also familiar with the supernatural world and came to her own conclusion about me.

"Alec Harbinger," she said as if she had known me all her life. "The preternatural investigator."

I'd been startled before but now I was taken aback. How did she know who I was? "Did you read my mind?"

"No," she said, shaking her head. Her long raven hair tumbled over her shoulders. "I read your advertisement. It was in the local newspaper."

"Ah, of course. And you are?"

"Victoria Blackwell." She offered a lace-gloved hand. "My sister Devon and I own Blackwell's Books. You must come by sometime for tea. We have many books in our shop that might interest you."

"Good to know," I said, shaking her hand. "Maybe I'll drop by sometime and take a look."

"Yes, I'm sure we'll see you soon." She smiled and walked onto Main Street, turning left and heading down the street. I took a right turn toward my office but stopped before going inside. I watched Victoria Blackwell's black-clad figure strolling along the sidewalk. Everyone in her vicinity gave her a wide berth and I guessed that even though those people didn't believe in witchcraft beyond what they saw in movies or read in books, they instinctively sensed something "different" about the Blackwell sisters.

Victoria disappeared through the door of an antiquated-looking building that had a sign reading BLACKWELL'S BOOKS over the door. I wondered if I'd underestimated the amount of preternatural activity in Dearmont. Witches tended to stick to areas where there were places of natural magical power, so if there were two witches running the bookshop in town, there was probably more to Dearmont than met the eye.

I went inside and ascended the stairs to meet my new client.

CHAPTER 9

I GOT TO THE TOP of the stairs and went into my office, walking past the bespectacled young man who was now sitting in a chair outside Felicity's office and looking like he might throw up at any moment. His face was ashen, his eyes darting nervously behind the thick-rimmed glasses.

Felicity came into my office as I was settling into my seat behind the desk. She closed the door behind her.

"What's with that guy out there?" I asked her. "He looks like he's seen a ghost."

"He's seen a monster." She handed me a cup of coffee. "His name is Timothy Ellsworth. He thinks he's been bitten by a werewolf."

"Werewolf? Why does he think that?"

She shrugged. "That's all he would tell me."

I sighed, hoping this was going to be a case that would fill our coffers and not just the ramblings of some guy who got bitten by a dog in the woods. "Okay, bring him in."

Felicity opened the door and called him in.

Timothy Ellsworth came into the office and sat in the chair opposite me. The T-shirt he wore was an old Rush T-shirt and it looked too big for his scrawny frame, as if he had lost weight recently. "Timothy," I said, "I'm Alec Harbinger. How can I help you?"

"I don't know if you can," he said. His voice was high-pitched, scared. "I've been bitten by a werewolf. Can you cure me? Can you lift the curse?"

"Do you know much about werewolves?"

He nodded, his glasses slipping down the bridge of his nose. "Yeah, I know some things." He pushed the glasses back up to where they belonged.

"Okay, tell me what happened." I sat back and gave him all the time he needed.

"This all happened three weeks ago," he said. "I've been going crazy since then because nobody will believe it was a werewolf that bit me. Everyone said it must have been a dog or a raccoon or something, but I know what I saw. Then I saw that you were opening a preternatural investigation office here in town and I knew if anyone would believe me, it'd be you. You believe me, right?"

"You haven't told me what happened yet," I said patiently. Whatever had happened to Timothy, it was wreaking havoc on his nerves. I was willing to listen, but I would reserve judgement until I'd heard the whole story.

"But you must know about werewolves," he said. "You know they exist, right? I'm not crazy."

I could see he was going to need some guidance to tell his story. "Where were you bitten?" I asked him.

"Right here," he said, lifting the Rush T-shirt to show me a nasty-looking wound along his ribs. It had been stitched and was covered with a dark brown scab. "See, that isn't a raccoon bite, or a dog bite either."

"It's difficult to tell," I said. "What did they say at the hospital when they stitched it up?"

"They just said it was some kind of animal. I had to have a course of rabies shots. But no shots can lift the werewolf curse." He frowned and then asked hopefully, "Can they?"

"No, rabies shots can't lift the curse of the werewolf," I told him.

"So I still have it. I'm still cursed. When the moon is full…."

"Where did this happen?" I asked, guiding him again.

"In our back yard. We live out on Cowper's Lane at the edge of town."

"We?" I asked.

"Me and my mom."

"Did she see what bit you?"

"No, she doesn't get out of bed much. She's ill. The doctors say it's depression because my dad died a couple of years ago. She never got over that. I'm all she has now. I look after her." His eyes widened in horror. "I can't be a werewolf. What'll happen to my mom?"

"Tell me how you got bit," I said, bringing him back on course.

He nodded and took a moment to calm himself as best he could. "We were watching Family Feud on TV and we heard a noise in the backyard. It sounded like, I don't know, like there was a dog out there or something like that. But it wasn't a dog," he added quickly.

"So you went out to investigate?"

"Yeah, but first I went down to the basement to get my dad's shotgun. I thought that if it was some kind of animal, I could scare it away. We have a cat, Mr. Picard, and I didn't want him to get eaten by something bigger than him. He's been in fights before, mainly with other cats, and he doesn't always win. He once had a fight with Marmalade—that's Mrs. Green's ginger cat from down the street—and…."

"You went outside with the shotgun," I reminded him.

"Yeah, I went outside with the shotgun," he said, getting back on track. "It was a quiet night and the noise in the yard had stopped by the time I got out there. I could hear Mr. Tobin's dog, Belle, barking at the end of the street, but it sounded far away. The moon was full, of course, and the yard was lit by the moonlight, but I couldn't see what had been making the noise. So I walked over to the woodpile and took a look behind it." He swallowed. "And that's when I saw it."

He stopped and put his hand to his mouth, trying to hold back tears but failing. They ran down his gaunt cheeks and landed on the Rush T-shirt, making wet stains in the fabric. Whatever had happened to Timothy that night, it was painful for him to relive the memory.

"You're safe now," I told him. "Describe to us what you saw behind the woodpile."

"It was horrible. A monster. It leaped out at me and sunk its teeth into my side."

"Did you get a good look at it?"

He nodded. "It's head was like a wolf but not exactly. It looked more … evil. Its eyes glowed like no wolf I've ever seen."

"Did it move on two legs like a human?" I asked.

"Yeah, it did. When I fell backward and hit the ground, I fired the shotgun and that woke up the entire neighborhood. People started coming out of their houses and the werewolf got spooked, I guess, and ran away. It ran on two legs like a human being. But it wasn't human; it was a monster. It disappeared into the trees behind the house. Mr. Ericsson from next door drove me to the hospital. I told him what I saw, but he said it was probably just a big dog that jumped out and surprised me and my mind filled in the rest because I watch too many horror movies."

His story sounded genuine enough, but there was only one way to know without a shadow of doubt if he'd been bitten by a werewolf or not. I made a mental calculation about the phases of the moon. It had just passed its first quarter, which meant the next full moon would be six nights from tonight. I consulted my desk calendar. "The next full moon is on Monday. I can take you to a location far away from town and observe you. I'll have to restrain you for your own safety."

Timothy frowned. "Don't you mean for your safety? If I turn into a werewolf, you'll be the one in danger."

"No," I said, shaking my head. "If you turn into a werewolf and you aren't restrained, I'll have to kill you. If you're in restraints, we're good."

"But what then? If I'm a werewolf, you'll have to kill me anyway, won't you?" He stumbled to his feet. "I need to leave. I thought you'd know how to lift the curse." He reached for the door handle.

"Come back here if you want to live," I told him.

He paused, his hand slowly retreating from the door. He turned to face me but said nothing.

"I can't let you leave here, knowing that you might be a lycanthrope," I said. "Sit down."

His eyes darted from me to Felicity to the chair. Slowly, he came back to it and sat down. "Oh my God, you're going to kill me," he said. Tears welled in his eyes.

"Have you killed anyone while in werewolf form?" I asked him.

He shook his head. "No, I haven't changed into werewolf form yet."

"So why the hell would I kill you?"

Timothy shrugged.

"You can't escape the curse," I told him. "But I can help you manage it. Every full moon, my assistant or myself will collect you from your home and take you to a secure location where you'll be locked away so you can't hurt anyone. We'll leave you at the location overnight and return in the morning to take you back home."

"That's it?" he asked. "That's all I have to do?"

"There will be a fee involved, of course."

He nodded enthusiastically, as if suddenly deciding that being a werewolf wasn't so bad after all. "That's not a problem. I have money."

"If you go with my assistant to her office, she'll fill out the necessary paperwork."

He got up and shook my hand. His bony grip was weak but I knew that if he wolfed out, he'd have enough strength to rip a man's heart out.

"Just one more thing," I said. "Make sure you're available on the days of the full moon. If I come to your house and you're not there, I will have to hunt you down."

"I understand," he said. Felicity took him out of the office.

I went to the window and looked out over Main Street. My first day in Dearmont had turned out a hell of a lot different from how I had imagined it this morning. I had a faerie kidnapping case, a possible werewolf victim, and I'd been attacked by ogres. How many more surprises was this town going to throw at me before the day was over?

I checked my watch. It was after four. Maybe I should call it a day and go get some food for the barbecue and a couple of cases of beer. I needed to unwind for a while and then think about who had sent those ogre assassins to kill me and why.

Felicity came into the office. "Everything is sorted out with Timothy Ellsworth. He's paid two months in advance."

"Good. Providing security services to werewolves means a steady paycheck. I had half a dozen werewolf clients in Chicago. Every full moon, I locked them up in a warehouse by the river in Joliet. It's easy money until one of them tries to take a bite out of you."

"And what about the other werewolf? The one that bit Timothy? It's still out there somewhere."

I turned from the window to look at her. "Yeah, I'm going to have to deal with that."

"How are you going to find it? Do you have to wait until it murders someone during the next full moon?"

"That's one option, but it means dealing with the police, something I want to avoid. Also, it means someone has to get killed before we can pick up the werewolf's trail. There's an easier way to find out if someone in town is cursed."

She raised a questioning eyebrow. "What's that?"

"There are a couple of witches in town, the Blackwell sisters. They own the bookshop down the street. The werewolf curse is magical in origin, so the witches should be able to cast a locator spell that leads to the cursed person."

"And when you find them, are you going to...?" She made a cutting motion across her throat.

"Not necessarily. If the cursed person has killed people while in werewolf form, then it's my job to send him to doggy heaven, but if he hasn't hurt anyone yet, I could offer him the same deal I offered Timothy. I was checking the local news reports earlier and there was nothing about dead bodies found after the full moon, so maybe this is a newly-turned werewolf whose only act of aggression so far was to bite Timothy."

"Or it could be that the killings happened elsewhere and the werewolf has recently moved to this area."

"Yeah, that's a possibility too."

"When are you going to see the witches?"

"Maybe tomorrow morning before we head off to the lake."

Felicity's dark eyes widened as if she was suddenly remembering something. "Should I see if I can rent one of those cabins for us to stay in?"

"Yeah, maybe you should. Get it for a few days if you can. There's a time dilation between Faerie and our world. It depends which part of the faerie realm I end up in, but I could spend what I think are a few hours there and days could pass here."

She nodded. "I'll make sure to bring some provisions."

"Speaking of provisions, let's call it a day here and I'll get some food for the barbecue."

"All right," she said, that pretty smile playing over her lips. "I'll just finish up a few things and then I'll head home."

"Just come over whenever you're ready," I said. "I'll have the barbecue all fired up." I followed her out of the office and into the hallway. She went into her own office and began typing on her keyboard. "Where's the nearest store?" I asked.

She gave me directions to a general store on Main Street and I left the office, deciding to walk there. It was still warm, but not uncomfortably so, and a stroll along Main Street, I thought, might give me a better feel for the town of Dearmont. My initial impression, that this was a preternatural dead zone, was obviously incorrect.

As I passed Blackwell Books, I peered in through the window to see Victoria Blackwell and a woman who was obviously her sister—same long, dark hair and similar black dress—serving customers among bookshelves that reached to the shop's ceiling.

I wondered if I should go in and ask them about the werewolf locator spell but decided against it. That could wait. There were still six nights to the full moon. Besides, the bookshop was too busy at the moment for me to go in there and talk about a possible monster in town. It might be quieter in the morning, giving me a chance to talk to the witches without scaring the good folk of Dearmont in the process.

An hour later, I was driving on to my street with sacks of food and cases of beer in the back of the Land Rover and a growing hunger in my belly. As I got closer to the house, I saw a figure sitting on the front stoop. Squinting against the sun, I could make out long auburn hair, hazel eyes, and, beneath her white summer dress, a physique that was slim but radiated a sense of inner strength. When I realized who it was, I felt a grin crack my face. The same moment I recognized Mallory, she saw the Land Rover and stood up, waving.

I pulled on to the driveway and cut the engine. Mallory was waiting to greet me as I opened the door and got out. She jumped into my arms and kissed my cheek. The familiar feel of her body against mine was arousing but also rekindled memories of frustration.

"When did you get here?" I asked her.

"About a half hour ago. I was going to wait in my Jeep but it's too damn hot so I thought I'd sit by your front door and give your neighbors something to look at." She gestured to the houses on the street. "Is this place quiet or what? I never thought I'd see you outside of the Windy City."

"You know I didn't have a choice."

She broke away from me and a serious look crossed her features. "Yeah, I know. Looks like they really screwed you over for what happened in Paris."

"It's not so bad," I said, trying to sound upbeat. "I thought this place would be dead but I have a couple of cases already."

"Cool. And a couple of cases of beer too, I see. You want some help getting those inside?"

"Of course." I opened the back of the Land Rover and passed her a case of Coors Light. "We're having a barbecue later, so how does burgers and hot dogs sound?"

"Sounds great." Then she eyed me suspiciously and said, "We?"

"Felicity Lake," I said. "She's my assistant."

Mallory grinned. "Is she pretty?"

"Yeah, I guess."

"You guess?" She swung her elbow against my arm playfully. "Maybe that's why you like it here in the boondocks, hmm?"

I grabbed a case of beer and took it to the front door, balancing it precariously on my raised knee while I fumbled with my keys. "It's nothing like that. There are too many complications in my life at the moment to add a relationship into the mix."

"Oh," she said with a mock pout. "What about your relationship with me?"

"That's one of the complications." I got the door open and entered the house, glad I had turned on the AC this morning. Walking out of the late afternoon warmth and into the cool house was refreshing.

"Don't let me stand in the way of you and your lovely assistant," Mallory said as we dumped the beers on to the kitchen table. "You know that what happens between you and me is nothing more than therapy."

"Yeah, I know." We went back out to the Land Rover to get the rest of the supplies.

"Why do you have an assistant anyway?" Mallory asked me. "You never had one before."

"The Society sent her here to spy on me."

"Oh, wow, they really don't trust you, do they?"

"You don't know the half of it," I said. "Remind me to tell you about the ogre assassins."

Her hazel eyes went wide. "Ogre assassins!" She realized she had said that out loud in the street and dropped her voice to a whisper. "Ogre assassins?"

"Yeah, like I said, this town isn't dead, but someone in the Society wants me to be. Anyway, what have you been doing since I last saw you?"

She shrugged, her face looking suddenly serious. "I've been traveling here and there. New York, Boston, the Florida Keys."

"The Florida Keys? Was that a vacation?" I handed her a case of beer.

"No," she said, shaking her head. "I can't take a vacation until he's dead, Alec. I can't live a normal life, have a normal relationship, until I know he's gone and never coming back. You know that." She took the beer into the house.

"Yeah," I said to myself, watching Mallory step through the front door and wondering if she would ever find the man who had ruined her life and taken so many others. She was touchy about it, but I couldn't blame her. All of her friends and classmates had been murdered five years ago during a high school party, an event the newspapers called the Bloody Summer Night Massacre. Some of the victims' bodies had been carved up with a knife, magical symbols cut into their flesh, and the guy who had done all the killing, a guy who referred to himself as Mister Scary, was still out there somewhere.

Mallory Bronson had been the only survivor that night and had been dubbed a Final Girl by the internet news sites, in reference to slasher movies where a single girl survives and beats the killer.

Mallory had beaten Mister Scary. She had shot him five times and knocked him over the safety railing of a third floor balcony, avenging the deaths of her classmates, or so she thought. But by the time the police arrived at Blackthorn House, where the massacre took place, Mister Scary had disappeared.

Just like in a slasher movie.

And Mallory had spent the past five years searching for him, following leads and unsolved murders all over the country. The emotional scars she carried weren't going to heal until the killer was dead. Mallory was sure that the death of the killer would allow her to forget her bloody past and move on, but I wasn't so sure it was that simple.

I grabbed a case of beer and followed her into the cool house.

CHAPTER 10

AN HOUR LATER, MALLORY AND I were sitting out back on foldout chairs I had found in the basement. It was a perfect area for training, with a hook already in place for my heavy bag and more than enough room to set up my weapons rack and training dummies. It even had a small bathroom, complete with a shower stall.

A small storage room led off the main basement area and that was where I had found the chairs and a white plastic table that the previous owners had left behind. There was even a large black and white striped umbrella that fitted through the hole in the center of the table and provided us with some shade.

The barbecue was throwing off charcoal-scented heat, the air above the grill shimmering. I'd told Mallory about the events of the day, including the ogre assassins. Now, we sat drinking beer while she tried to figure out who would want to kill me.

"It has to be someone in the Inner Circle," she said.

"Yeah, but no one knows who the members of the Inner Circle are," I reminded her.

"We know your father is a member. Maybe he can tell you."

"Are you kidding? He would never do that. As far as he's concerned, the Society's secrets are more important than his own life, never mind mine."

Mallory put her beer on the table and pressed her thumb and forefinger to her temples as if it would help her think. "Okay, let's look at this from a different angle. Instead of trying to figure out who's in the Inner Circle, let's try to figure out why someone from the Inner Circle would want you dead."

"Because of what happened in Paris," I said.

"And what exactly happened in Paris?" Felicity's voice came from the side of the house, where it was possible to walk from the street to the backyard where we were sitting. She was holding a bottle of red wine in one hand and she had changed into jeans and a dark blue t-shirt with the Coca Cola logo across the swell of her breasts. Her dark hair, which had been piled up earlier, was scraped back into a ponytail, accentuating the feminine lines of her face. She waved at us as she approached.

"The lovely assistant, I presume," Mallory whispered.

I kicked her chair, but not too hard, because I knew how easily those damned things folded up on themselves.

Felicity came over and set the bottle of wine on the table among the packages of meat and buns.

"Felicity, this is my friend Mallory Bronson," I said. "Mallory, this is Felicity my … assistant." I mentally kicked myself for almost saying *lovely assistant*. "I'll get some wine glasses," I said, excusing myself and going into the kitchen to search the cupboards. All of my cups, mugs, glasses, and plates had been unpacked and put into the kitchen cupboards when I'd arrived at the house. At the time, I'd wondered who had done that, but now I knew it was Felicity. Maybe her efficiency at arranging my stuff and unpacking some of my boxes had been borne of guilt. After all, she'd been sent here to spy on me.

I found three wine glasses and a corkscrew and went back outside. Felicity busied herself with opening the wine while I arranged three burgers on the grill. They sizzled juicily and the charcoal briquettes sent up little plumes of smoke as the fat hit them.

"God, that smells good," Mallory said.

"Nothing like a burger cooked over a barbecue," I said.

Felicity was pouring the wine. "Are you two avoiding my question?"

Mallory and I looked at each other. I had not heard Felicity ask a question. "What's that?" I asked.

"When I got here, you were talking about Paris. I asked you what happened there." She turned her attention to

Mallory and handed her a glass of wine. "Do you know what happened in Paris?"

Mallory nodded. "Yeah, of course."

"Of course," Felicity repeated softly. I wondered if she was trying to figure out whether my relationship with Mallory was more than mere friendship.

I flipped the burgers. As they were turned over, a new bout of sizzling and spitting began. I turned to Felicity. "What happened in Paris should have never have happened at all. I wasn't even supposed to be there. Not on a job, anyway. It was supposed to be a vacation."

"A vacation, how nice," Felicity said. "I love Paris."

"Anyway," I said, "I was in Paris taking a break. We're allowed to take one now and then, but not often enough. I usually spent my vacations in Chicago, but that never worked out because there would always be a call or a message from someone who needed something. Or the guy temping my job while I was away would need help and I'd end up not taking a break at all. So I decided to get out of the country and go to Paris. I thought that being so far away meant I'd be left alone for a while. It didn't turn out that way.

"I'd only been there a couple of days when my father called me. He said he needed me to do something urgently for the Society. It was a simple job. All I had to do was check on the Paris investigator in the area of the city where I was staying. Pierre Louvain. I was to make sure Pierre was okay and report back to my father."

"Did he say why?" Felicity asked.

"No, he just told me to check on him."

"So why didn't your father send one of the other Paris investigators to check on Pierre?" she asked.

"Oh, believe me, I asked him. I told him I was on vacation, it was the middle of the night, and if he wanted someone to check on this guy he needed to send someone else, like any of the other investigators in the city. He said that Pierre had called him and said that he couldn't trust anyone in the city. He thought the Society in Paris had been compromised by its enemies. So, since I was from out of town, it was decided that I should do some investigation into the matter. Like I said, I never get a real vacation."

I turned my attention back to the burgers. They were ready. I put three buns onto paper plates and opened them to begin assembling the burgers. "There's ketchup, mustard, BBQ sauce, and cheese slices; help yourselves," I said as I slid two of the plates across the table to Mallory and Felicity.

While they were fixing their burgers, I put some chicken thighs on the grill and took another sip of red wine.

"So, I had to go and check out this Pierre guy," I told Felicity. "I was pretty pissed at the Society for interrupting my vacation but I went over to where the guy's office anyway. I'd hired a Vespa scooter for the week I was there, which was ideal for getting around Paris, so I rode over there on that. When I got to Pierre's office, the place was a mess. Someone … or something … had trashed the place. If there had been anything there that would be useful, I figured it had been taken."

I put cheese, mustard, and ketchup on my burger and took a bite. It wasn't as good as the burger I'd had at Darla's Diner, but it was still delicious. "I had Pierre's home address, so I rode over there, wondering if the poor guy was dead or alive. I felt vulnerable. I had no idea what I was getting myself into and I had no weapons. If Pierre's message had been correct and the Society in Paris had been compromised, there was nobody I could turn to for help."

"You thought members of the Society were trying to kill one of the Society's investigators?" Felicity asked. "But why would they do that? Who could make them become traitors like that?"

"I don't know the answer to that," I said. "I got to Pierre's place, a nice first floor apartment near the Louvre, and found him there. He was dead. His throat had been slashed open and his tongue had been cut out. It was lying on the floor near his body."

Felicity put down her wine. "Oh my God, that's terrible."

"Yeah. I called my father and told him what I'd found. He decided to tell me what this was all about. I guess he figured that if I found Pierre alive and well, my involvement would end there and I could finish my vacation in peace. But now that I'd discovered Pierre's body, I might as well be told what was going on. I was in deep now."

I paused to turn the chicken thighs on the barbecue. The smell rising up from them made me hungry despite the half-eaten burger on my plate and the memory of Pierre Louvain's body lying in his apartment in a pool of dark blood.

I returned to the table and leaned over the buns and mustard to talk to Felicity in a lower voice. News travels fast in small towns and I didn't want a nosy neighbor to overhear me and tell the rest of the street that the new guy belonged to a secret society that had its roots in sixteenth century Europe and was at war with supernatural forces all over the world. It might make small talk difficult when I was mowing my front lawn.

"Pierre Louvain had been investigating a Japanese woman in Paris who might be a *satori*." I took a bite of my burger.

"I've heard of those," Felicity said. "They read minds and predict the future."

"Yeah, they're very rare." I used the barbecue tongs to get the thighs from the grill to a paper plate. "They're usually only found in Japan and they're shunned by society there, forced to live in the mountains. A lot of people think they can control other people's minds as well as read them, which makes *satoris* feared."

"And there was one in Paris?" Felicity took a chicken thigh and put it on her plate to cool down.

I nodded. "My father told me that Pierre Louvain had discovered a possible *satori*. A *satori* would be very valuable to the Society because of the alleged mind control powers they possess. For the same reason, a *satori* would also be valuable to the Society's enemies. So Pierre reported his findings to the Society's London headquarters, thinking they'd want to send over some people to talk the *satori* into working for them."

"But it didn't turn out that way?" Felicity asked.

"No, it didn't. After making the call, Pierre kept watch over the woman. Only a couple of hours after he had informed headquarters about her, a number of Paris investigators arrived at her apartment and kidnapped her. They bundled her into the back of a van and drove away. Pierre said the investigators were working with vampires. He followed the van on his motorcycle and called headquarters again, asking what the hell was going on. He was told that the Society hadn't sanctioned the kidnapping of the *satori* and were still putting together a team of people to fly over to Paris to speak with her."

"So," Mallory said, biting into a chicken thigh, "someone at headquarters found out about the message and decided to act on it themselves."

"But who would do that?" Felicity asked.

"Someone who wanted to bag themselves a *satori*," Mallory said through a mouthful of chicken.

"It has to be a member of the Inner Circle," I said. "If the Society thought there was a *satori* in Paris, that information would be restricted to the highest level members. My father only told me because I was directly involved in a possible rescue mission."

Felicity frowned. "But how could you be? Pierre was dead, so how could you know where they'd taken the *satori*?"

"When the van reached its destination, Pierre called my father and left a four-word message before the line went dead. He said, '*L'empire de la mort.*' After that, he wasn't seen or heard from again until I found his body in his apartment. They must have taken him back there to kill him."

"*L'empire de la mort*," Felicity said. "The empire of the dead."

"Yeah, there's an inscription over the entrance to the Paris catacombs that says, 'Stop! This is the empire of the dead.' I'd visited the catacombs the day before, so I knew what Pierre was referring to. My father knew, too, but his team were still in England and I was the only Society member he trusted in Paris, so I had to go to the catacombs and rescue the *satori* from the corrupt investigators and vampires.

"I searched Pierre's apartment and found a dagger and a few stakes and took them out to the Vespa. I didn't have a plan other than going into the catacombs and killing anyone or anything that wasn't the *satori*. Great vacation, huh?"

The frown on Felicity's face told me she was confused about something. "What is it?" I asked her.

"Something doesn't make sense. You were kicked out of your Chicago office and sent here because of what happened in Paris, yet you were acting in your father's orders. You were doing what was best for the Society. Why did they punish you for that?"

"I didn't exactly follow orders. When I got to the catacombs, I took out two vampire guards posted at the street entrance and descended into the underground caves. I had to go a long way into the skull-lined catacombs before I found the *satori* and her captors. The captors were already dead, their bodies lying in a mess on the ground, blood coming out of their ears and their eyes. The *satori* had done that somehow with her power. I guess they hadn't thought their kidnapping plan through. The *satori* was standing among the dead bodies, calmly looking at me as I entered the area. She looked just like any other young Japanese woman, dressed in jeans and a hoodie that wasn't even blood-stained, despite the carnage around her."

Felicity was frowning again.

"What is it?" I asked her.

"If the *satori* could kill the vampires and rogue agents at any time, why did she wait until they took her to the catacombs? Why not just kill them in her apartment? Or in the van?"

I shrugged. "I have no idea. And I wasn't going to question her about it. She'd just taken out a small army with the power of her mind."

"I guess she had her reasons for waiting," Mallory said.

"So what happened next?" Felicity asked.

I hesitated. The next part of the story was a blur. After returning to my hotel room in Paris, I'd searched my memory, trying to fit all the pieces together, to remember exactly what had happened after I'd discovered the *satori* in the catacombs, but I could never seem to recall everything clearly.

"This is where it all gets a little hazy," I told Felicity. "I think the *satori* may have made me forget something that happened. What I remember is that her name was Sumiko. I don't remember her telling me that, but I know that's her name somehow. We left the catacombs and I told her to flee the city. I told her to get as far away as possible so that the Society couldn't find her."

Felicity was nodding as if suddenly understanding something. "So that's why you got in trouble. Instead of talking the *satori* into joining the Society, you told her to run."

"I couldn't have talked her into anything. And I now knew that the Society was corrupt at its highest level. I couldn't let them get their hands on her. Someone in the Inner Circle wanted to use her for his own ends."

"Or her own ends," Mallory said.

"Or her own ends. I have no idea if the corrupt member of the Inner Circle is a man or a woman. There might be more than one of them, for all I know. The only thing I know for sure is that they're now trying to kill me and I have no idea why."

Mallory threw a chicken bone on to her plate. "It's obvious, Alec. They think you know who they are, that you're a danger to them in some way. Why else would risk dealing with faeries and possibly blowing their cover?"

"But I don't know anything."

"But they don't know that," she said, taking another chicken thigh and biting into it. "Maybe they think the rogue investigators told you who they were working for. You might know the names of everyone in the Inner Circle who's corrupt."

I shook my head. "I was questioned about all this. After I left the catacombs and went back to my hotel, the Society sent people to France to 'escort' me to headquarters in London. I was debriefed. They put an iron collar around my neck while they questioned me. It was an enchanted relic from the Spanish Inquisition and it made me tell the truth. I told them everything I know, everything I just told you and Felicity. There's nothing else."

"Nothing that you can remember, anyway," Felicity said.

"I admit some of my memory is fuzzy, but I'm not hiding anything."

"Not that you know of," Mallory said, pointing a chicken bone at me. "If the *satori* played around with your memory, you might know stuff that you aren't even aware of."

"Great. So I'm going to be killed for something I can't even remember?"

Mallory laughed. "Yeah, that's the way the world works, Alec. You get shafted for something that isn't even your fault."

We ate for a while, the subject of Paris closed, as far as I was concerned. If there was something I couldn't remember about that night in the catacombs, it was probably going to stay locked inside my head forever.

"How did you two meet?" Felicity asked eventually. I'd wondered when she was going to get around to asking that.

I looked at Mallory. "Do you want to tell the story?"

She shrugged. "Sure. There's really not much to tell. A couple of years ago, Alec and I sort of bumped into one another at a crime scene in Chicago. The bodies of two high school students, a boy and a girl, were found in Millennium Park. They'd been murdered and the killer had inscribed occult symbols into their flesh with a knife. So, that explains why Alec was there. My reason for being there may take a little more explaining. Have you ever heard of the Bloody Summer Night Massacre?"

Felicity nodded. "Yes, of course. It was five or six years ago. Some high school students were having a party at an abandoned house and they all got killed."

"Not all of them." Mallory pushed her plate away and drained her wine glass before continuing. "I survived."

"Oh, yes, now I remember. There was a girl who survived. That was you?"

Mallory nodded.

"The newspapers had a name that they gave you. The Last Girl."

"The Final Girl," Mallory said. "That's the term used for the girl who survives to the end of a slasher movie. You know, the girl who sees all her friends die and then takes on the killer."

"And that's what happened to you? You saw all your friends die? That's horrible." Felicity put a comforting hand on Mallory's. "That must have affected you in ways I can't even imagine."

"Yeah," Mallory said. "The point is, the bastard who killed everyone, except for me, that night is still out there somewhere. I thought I'd killed him, but he got away. I've been hunting him ever since."

"So that's why you were at the crime scene," Felicity guessed.

"Yeah, and that's where Alec and I met. It turned out that the killings weren't done by my guy and they weren't preternatural either. The killer was just some high school kid who'd read too many books about black magic and hated his classmates. But Alec and I worked together on that case for a while and we've stayed in touch ever since. He even hired me to work a couple of preternatural cases with him as a consultant."

"Mallory is good with people," I said. "Especially people who've lost their loved ones. I took her to meet some victims' families when I was working a big vampire case. She helped me break the bad news that their loved ones were dead."

"I kicked some vampire butt too," she added.

"Yes, you did." To Felicity, I said, "Mallory has spent the five years since the Bloody Summer Night Massacre training in hand-to-hand and weapons combat. She's pretty kickass."

"Sounds like you two make a great team," Felicity said. Was that a hint of jealousy I detected in her voice? She looked at her phone. "I really should be heading home. We're getting an early start tomorrow aren't we, Alec? It's a three-hour drive to Dark Rock Lake."

"I have to go to the bookshop first," I said, "so we don't need to leave here until, say, ten or eleven. Did you rent a cabin?"

"Yes, I got a three-day rental." She checked the phone again. "Anyway, I need to get home for when Jason video calls me. He's in England, so it's already late evening for him."

"Jason?" I asked.

"My boyfriend."

118

I nodded. "Okay."

"Do you have far to go?" Mallory asked her. "To get home, I mean."

"No," Felicity said, getting to her feet. "I live next door." To me, she added, "I'll see you in the office when you're done at the bookshop." She looked at Mallory again. "Nice to meet you, Mallory."

"See you tomorrow," I called to her as she disappeared around the side of the house.

Mallory looked at me. "She lives next door? Well, that's convenient." She flashed me a wicked grin.

I shot her a look that told her I wasn't amused. "Don't even go there. Anyway, you heard what she said: she has a boyfriend."

"Yeah, and he's all the way across the ocean in England while you're right next door."

I looked at her and shook my head. "Felicity and I are work colleagues. I'm helping her get experience in the field so she can become an investigator."

"And you're going to a cabin by the lake for three days as part of this experience?" She winked at me.

"I told you, we're going to look for James Robinson and Sarah Silverman. Their bodies are probably up there somewhere in an enchanted sleep. I'm going to travel to Faerie to see if I can locate their trapped souls. There's a time dilation between Faerie and here, so days might pass here while I'm away."

"Well, be sure to get back here by the full moon because you need to lock up that werewolf you told me about. And track down the werewolf that bit him. Or do you want me to handle that while you take your assistant on the lake retreat?"

"You sticking around for awhile?" I asked her. You could never tell with Mallory. Sometimes she'd stay for a week, and other times, she'd disappear after a few hours.

She nodded. "Yeah, I think I will. You might need me."

"Great. You can come to see the witches with me tomorrow and work the werewolf angle while Felicity and I go find those bodies. How does that sound?"

"It sounds fine, but there's something I want you to do for me, too."

I knew what she was going to say and it made me both excited and anxious at the same time. Excited because of what we were going to do, but anxious because we had been doing it for two years and I wasn't sure it was helping Mallory at all. "Therapy?" I asked.

She nodded. "Therapy."

"Do you think it'll be any different to last time?"

She thought about it for a couple of seconds and then said, "I think I'll be able to go farther than last time."

"Okay. You want to do it now or…."

"Later," she said. "When it's dark. It has to be when it's dark."

* * *

Later, when night fell, we went wordlessly up to my bedroom and stood facing each other by the bed. Mallory's breathing had already quickened and in the silvery moonlight that came in through the window, I could see her breasts rising and falling with each rapid breath. I couldn't fool myself into thinking that her fast breathing was due to excitement. I knew she was afraid.

In every slasher flick, there's a lesson that the poor victims of the killer learn too late: sex equals death. Every couple that makes out in those movies ends up dead, as if being punished for their carnal desires. For Mallory, the sex equals death equation wasn't just something she'd seen in the movies; she had seen it happen in real life. All of the high school kids who had paired off and ventured into the bedrooms of Blackthorn House had met a grisly end at the hands of Mister Scary. The idea that having sex was deadly had been carved into the deepest recesses of Mallory's mind.

After she and I had become friends, she'd confided in me that the thought of having sex filled her with dread and even though she knew on a rational level that her fear was ludicrous, an irrational part of her would not let her give in to desire.

The therapists she visited regularly couldn't help her, no matter how much they tried to rationalize her fear and help her overcome it. After the therapists failed to help her, Mallory told me that the only way she could be cured was by practical means. She had to try having sex, and it had to be with someone she trusted and who would understand that the experiment was purely for therapeutic reasons and had no emotional baggage attached to it.

At first, I had jumped at the chance. Mallory was a beautiful young woman in her early twenties and her offer was the stuff of many a man's wet dream. But when I saw how deep and powerful her fear was, I spent the "therapy" sessions worrying about Mallory's mental state. I wasn't sure this was the best way for her to be cured and I told her so on more than one occasion. Each time, she convinced me to continue with the sessions, saying there was no one else she trusted enough to take over my role.

So here I was, standing in front of her in a dark bedroom while she almost hyperventilated with fear.

I moved toward her slowly, reaching my hands up to touch her bare arms. Her scared hazel eyes shone in the moonlight as she looked up at me. Inwardly, I cursed Mister Scary for what he had done to my beautiful friend. She deserved better than this.

I bent my head down toward her and kissed her softly. She kissed me back, her eyes darting to the shadowy corners of the room as if she expected a killer to come bursting out of the darkness, brandishing the same knife he had used to carve up a group of high school kids five years ago.

"Do you want me to turn on the light?" I whispered.

"No, leave it," she said softly. "Undress me, Alec."

I hooked my thumbs under the dress straps and pulled them off her shoulders. Mallory wriggled her hips and the dress whispered down over her body to the floor. She began tugging at my T-shirt. I removed it and took Mallory into my arms, feeling her soft breasts pressing against my hard chest.

"Remember," I whispered to her, "we can stop any time you want."

"I know we can," she said. "That's why I trust you." Her finger traced over the outline of a magical protection tattoo on my torso. Her touch was light, her finger shaking. "Let's get on the bed."

We climbed on to the bed, Mallory holding me tight as if I were a life raft on rough seas. Her breathing was even quicker now and I wondered if there might be a hint of excitement among all the fear. I was excited, of course, but I tried not to think about that and to focus on Mallory's need instead.

I slid her panties down her sleek legs while she pulled my jeans down to my thighs. I kicked them off on to the floor. We were both naked. This was as far as Mallory had ever gone without having to stop, overwhelmed with terror.

She was trembling like a tiny leaf about to be blown away by a violent storm.

I nuzzled her neck, kissing her soft skin lightly. Mallory's head darted from left to right and back again as she tried to watch all the shadows in the room around us. I felt a scream rising inside her and before she could let it out, I moved my face away from her neck and looked into her eyes, keeping my arms around her. "Do you want to stop?"

She nodded, her eyes scanning the dark corners of the room, tears welling up in them, making them glisten in the moonlight.

Then she began to cry.

I held her close, whispering to her that everything was going to be okay. Eventually, she fell asleep in my arms. When I felt the slow and calm rise and fall of her breasts against my chest, I closed my eyes and allowed myself to fall asleep, too.

In my dreams. I searched an old abandoned house, looking for a killer known only as Mister Scary. I had my sword in hand and knew that when I found him, I was going to cut him in two.

CHAPTER 11

WHEN I WOKE THE NEXT morning, Mallory wasn't in bed beside me. I sat up, squinting against the sunlight pouring in through the window. I really needed to hang the drapes sometime soon. The smell of coffee drifted up from the kitchen and I could hear a noise somewhere in the house that sounded like a rhythmic thumping.

I swung my legs out of bed, put on my boxers, and went downstairs. In the kitchen, I found coffee in the pot and poured myself a mug full, which I took down the basement with me. That was where the noise was coming from.

I descended the wooden steps to find that Mallory had hung the heavy bag and was currently punching and kicking the shit out of it. The training dummies were scattered over the basement floor as if they had been hurled to their resting places. One of them had the hilt of a dagger protruding from its forehead. Another had two daggers embedded in its chest.

Mallory sensed my presence and turned to face me, wiping perspiration from her face. She was wearing a tight, black Tapout top and training pants which I assumed she'd gotten from the back of her Jeep. Because she traveled around so much, Mallory tended to take a lot of gear on her road trips.

"Hey," she said. "I'm just working off some steam."

"Yeah, I can see that. Looks like these guys got the worst of it." I nodded at the training dummies scattered over the floor.

She grinned. "Yeah, I used some of your weapons. I hope you don't mind."

"Not at all. You know you can use anything of mine."

A serious look crossed her features. "Alec, I feel like I'm using you, not just your stuff. Last night was a disaster. I thought it would be better than last time, but it wasn't any different. I hate that I put you through this shit every time I turn up."

"Hey," I said, going to her and putting a hand in her shoulder. "Don't worry about it. Making a big thing out of it is only going to make it harder the next time. You have enough to deal with without worrying how it's affecting me."

"Is it affecting you? Because if it is…."

126

"Nah," I said nonchalantly, "I'm cold as ice. Hard as rock."

"Well, yeah, hard as rock is the problem I'm talking about."

"I'm fine. You still up for going to see the witch sisters this morning?"

She nodded. "Of course, I'll do what I can to help. I should hit the shower first, though."

"Yes, you should. You've worked up quite a sweat."

"Want to join me?" she asked playfully. "You look a little hot and bothered yourself."

"Not me," I said, "I'm…."

"Yeah, yeah, I know, cold as ice," she said as she sashayed to the shower room, swinging her hips a little more than normal.

"And hard as rock," I said, sighing as I ascended the stairs, coffee in hand.

* * *

We got to Blackwell Books at just after nine. It was another sunny morning and Main Street was bustling with townsfolk going about their business. I'd left the Land Rover in the same parking space as yesterday and Mallory and I had walked down to the bookshop from there. She was dressed in tight jeans, a loose, light white sweater, and running shoes. I was in my usual jeans, T-shirt, red flannel shirt, and boots.

There were a couple of customers inside Blackwell Books when we pushed through the door into the gloomy, musty-smelling interior of the shop. The shop was large and seemed to consists of more than one room. Book shelves had been arranged in a haphazard fashion over the available floor space. Every wall had shelves running from floor to ceiling and every shelf groaned beneath the weight of paperback and hardback books, as well as occult items like fake skull candles and goddess statuettes. The Blackwell sisters obviously monetized their witchcraft. I just hoped the sisters weren't all style and no substance. My senses had told me otherwise when I'd bumped into Victoria Blackwell yesterday, but those same senses had told me that Dearmont was a preternatural dead zone, and that obviously wasn't true.

"Mr. Harbinger, it's good to see you."

I turned to see Victoria Blackwell coming over to us from behind the counter. She wore a black lace and velvet dress, the same as yesterday. The only thing missing from her ensemble was the black lace parasol.

"Hey," I said as she reached us. "This is my friend…."

"Mallory Bronson," Victoria said, shaking Mallory's hand. "I read all about you in the paper. That night at Blackthorn House was simply terrible. Would either of you like tea?"

"Umm, sure," I said. "Listen, I've come here to ask for your help with something."

She raised one eyebrow. "Oh? I thought that your Society forbade you to seek help from witches."

"It's frowned upon," I said. "It isn't forbidden."

She paused for a moment, as if thinking. Then she said, "All right. Come through to the back room and we can discuss terms." She led us through the maze of bookshelves toward the back of the building.

Mallory looked at me and silently mouthed, "Terms?"

I shrugged. I hadn't expected the witches to cast a locator spell for free, but the word "terms" seemed to suggest more than a monetary payment.

"Devon, would you like to join us in the back room for a moment?" Victoria asked her sister as we passed her among the shelves. Devon Blackwell's features were similar to Victoria's except she had a softer, younger face. I guessed that she might be in her mid-twenties while Victoria was four or five years older. Both sisters shared the same dark eyes, long raven hair, and sultry good looks.

We were taken through a door marked PRIVATE and into a room that was filled with stacks of boxes and packages. A small metal desk with a computer sat in the corner. "This is where we run the mail order part of our business," Victoria explained as we entered the room. "Please take a seat." There was an old leather sofa pushed against one wall with a long wooden coffee table in front of it. Mallory and I sat on the sofa while Victoria perched on the metal desk. Devon went to a kitchenette area and boiled water in an electric kettle while she spooned tea into a large ceramic tea pot.

"So, what is the nature of your problem?" Victoria asked.

"I think there's a werewolf in town," I said. "I don't want to have to wait for the full moon to find out who it is. By then, it might have killed somebody. I was hoping you could cast a locator spell that would tell me where the werewolf is."

Victoria pursed her lips. "To what end?"

"Whoever this person is, they might not even know they're a werewolf. I can offer them a safe, secure environment on the nights of the full moon. They won't have to worry that they're going to lose control and kill someone because of their curse."

"So you want to protect them."

"I want to protect them and I want to protect everyone else from them."

Devon came over with the tea, placing the pot and cups on the coffee table, along with sugar and milk. She began pouring the drinks.

Mallory asked her, "Aren't you worried that while you're both back here, your store is unattended?"

Devon smiled at Mallory as if she were looking at a small child. "No, that isn't a concern."

I grinned. There must be so many magical wards on this building that shoplifting wasn't an issue. Nobody was going to walk out of here with a book they hadn't paid for.

"We can perform a locator spell to find the werewolf," Victoria said. "The curse is a magical one, so we can hone in on it. The only question remaining concerns payment."

"I can pay you," I said. Even as I said the words, I was wondering how fast Felicity could send an expense claim to the Society of Shadow's headquarters and how quickly they would wire the money into my account.

"We don't have any need of your money," Devon said. "The bookshop and mail order service amply fulfils our needs in that respect."

"Okay," I said, "so what would you want from me?"

Victoria took a sip of tea. "We are providing you with a service, so we ask the same in return. An exchange of services. We provide you with magic, and in return, you provide us with your investigative skills."

I frowned. "Do you have something you need investigating?"

"Not at the moment, no."

"So you do this favor for me and then I owe you one," I said.

Victoria smiled. There was nothing predatory about it but I wondered what I would be required to do for these witches in the future. "Yes," she said. "We live in the same town, so we might as well work together, don't you think? This arrangement could be mutually beneficial for all of us."

I sighed. Did I really have a choice? If I didn't find out where that werewolf was and make sure it was locked up in six nights' time, when the moon was full, someone in this town might be murdered, ripped apart by claws and fangs.

"All right, let's do it. You cast the spell and I'll return the favor in the future." I took a sip of the tea and had to stop myself from spitting it right back out again. It was some sort of bitter concoction that tasted of cinnamon, lemons, and maybe fennel. I forced myself to swallow it. Nobody else seemed to have a problem with the taste. I vowed to stick to coffee from now on.

"We'll cast the spell tonight," Victoria said. "After we close. I'll come by your office tomorrow and let you know the results."

"The office will be closed tomorrow. I have to travel out of town later today and I'm not sure when I'll get back. Mallory will come to the bookshop and you can give the results to her. Oh, and when you cast the spell, if you locate a werewolf at Cowper's Lane, you can ignore it. We already know about that guy."

"Very well," Victoria said, standing. "We have a deal. Shall we shake on it?"

I didn't feel like sealing the deal I'd just made in any way, but if I wanted to know where that werewolf was, I had no choice. I shook Victoria's hand and did the same with her sister. As soon as our hands clasped, Devon's eyes widened, then rolled back into her head. I began to pull away from her grip, which had suddenly strengthened, but Victoria said, "No, keep the contact with her. She's having a vision. It's her gift."

I stood, watching, as Devon Blackwell, her eyes showing nothing but whites, began to tremble all over. "Is she okay?" I asked Victoria.

She held up a hand, telling me to be quiet.

Devon whispered something but the words were too low and raspy to make out.

Victoria leaned toward her sister and said, "What is it, Devon? What do you see?"

The words came rasping out of Devon's mouth again: "Empire of the dead."

CHAPTER 12

WHEN DEVON BLACKWELL FINALLY LET go of my hand, her eyes became normal again. She leaned heavily against a stack of boxes, trying to regain her composure.

"What the hell just happened?" I asked her.

"She has visions sometimes," Victoria said. "They come unbidden, especially if someone she touches has had a traumatic experience in their life or is under an enchantment."

I frowned. "I'd understand it if she'd touched Mallory and had a vision, but not me. I haven't had any traumatic experiences."

"Do you know what 'empire of the dead' means?"

"Yes, it means the catacombs in Paris. I was there recently. We were talking about it last night. Is that what she's picking up on? Nothing traumatic happened to me there."

Devon looked up at me. "It isn't trauma, it's an enchantment. There's a door in your mind that was put there to lock away a memory. I saw it, but I couldn't open it to see what lay beyond. Whatever memory was locked away has been replaced by an enchantment, a memory you think is real but isn't. It has something to do with the empire of the dead. That's all I could glean before I was thrown out of the vision."

"Okay, this is getting really creepy," I said. "I'm not under any enchantment. I'm protected from things like that. Look." I pulled up my shirt and T-shirt to show them the tattoos on my body.

"Those symbols can't protect you from everything," Victoria said dismissively. "Wait here." She left the room and came back a couple of minutes later with a talisman on a leather cord. The talisman seemed to be made of stone and had a rune engraved on its surface. Victoria held it near me and said, "Freyja, adept of the mysteries, open our eyes to the magic which has been hidden from our sight."

The rune-engraved stone began to spin, slowly at first and then gaining speed until it was spinning so fast it was a blur of motion. Victoria took it away from me and it stopped immediately. Putting the amulet into a pocket of her dress, Victoria said, "There's a spell on you, and judging by how fast the rune was spinning, it's a powerful enchantment."

"I'm fine, really," I said. I didn't feel enchanted, not that I'd have any idea what that felt like. Maybe this was a little parlor trick the witch sisters did to drum up business. First Devon did her vision act and then the spinning amulet came out. After telling some poor sucker that they'd been enchanted, the witches offered to remove said enchantment, for a price, of course.

But that didn't explain how Devon knew about the empire of the dead.

Besides, I didn't really think these two were charlatans, otherwise I wouldn't be here asking for their help with the werewolf locator spell.

"Would you like us to help you?" Victoria asked. "It would take some time to do the proper research, but...."

"I'm fine," I repeated. Locator spells were one thing but I didn't want any witches poking around inside my head. I left the room with Mallory on my heels, a concerned look on her face.

"Alec, are you sure you're okay?" She looked worried about me and I didn't like that at all. I didn't want anyone to feel like that toward me. I was the guy who fixed other people's problems without having any of his own. I was supposed to make everyone feel safe, not concerned.

"I'm totally fine," I said firmly as we left the shop. The fresh air on the street outside made me realize how pungent-smelling the Blackwell sisters' tea had been. "Did you try that tea?" I asked Mallory, in an attempt to start a new conversation with a subject other than myself. "Was that stuff disgusting or what?"

"It wasn't too bad," she said as we walked along the street toward my office. "The sisters are a bit oddball, though."

"Some witches are. It's because they spend so much time reading old books. Like, really old books."

"The bookshop was kind of cool," she said.

"You think so? It was like chaos theory in practice."

"Well, that's what makes it cool," she said. "You could walk among those shelves and never know what you might discover next."

"Probably a demon serving disgusting tea," I said. "That stuff was so bad, it had to be otherworldly." We reached the door to my office, the one that said HARBINGER P.I. on the glass panel, and went through.

When we got to the top of the stairs, Felicity poked her head out of her office and waved. She had her phone pressed to her ear and was saying, "Yes … fine … just a couple of cases," into it.

I took Mallory into my office. "Well, what do you think?"

She looked around and nodded. "Looks good. The Society got you a nice place here."

"Yeah, but it's probably bugged. They sent Felicity here to spy on me, but they probably bugged the office too. Maybe even the house."

She went to the window and looked out. "Oh, yeah, there's a black van parked across the street with tinted windows. Do they normally have all those aerials and antennae on the roof?"

"Very funny," I said.

"Well, one of us has to be, and it isn't going to be you. You've been in a bad mood since we left the bookshop. Are you worried about what they said? About you being enchanted? Because I am."

"Don't worry about me," I said.

"It's difficult not to after what those witches said. You saw how fast that rune thing was spinning. If that *satori* put some kind of mind mojo on you, who knows what actually happened in Paris? You don't, because you're remembering a memory that was placed in your head."

"It doesn't matter now," I said. "It's done and dusted. Whatever actually happened, I got slapped down by the Society and here I am."

She looked at me with a serious look on her face. "You don't want to know what really happened? That doesn't sound like the Alec Harbinger I know. The Alec Harbinger I know loves a mystery and is great at solving them. Where's that guy, huh?"

"Back in Chicago."

She let out a groan of frustration. "You can be very annoying at times, you know that?"

"It's part of my charm."

"No," she said, shaking her head. "It really isn't."

Felicity came into the office. She was wearing hiking boots, jeans, and a black hoodie over a white T-shirt. Her hair was scraped back into a ponytail, the same as it had been last night at the barbecue. "That was your father on the phone, Alec."

"Oh? What did dear old Dad want?"

"He asked me how things were on your first day and if you were settling into your new home."

"Did you tell him we're going faerie hunting?"

"I told him about the Robinson case and the Ellsworth case. I didn't mention the ogres that tried to kill us. I thought I'd leave that up to you."

I nodded. "I'll tell him about that when I know more information, like who sent them. There's no point in telling him anything until I know who's behind it all, pulling the strings."

"You're probably right," Felicity said. "How did it go with the witches?"

"Great," I said, shooting Mallory a look that told her not to say anything. "They're going to cast the locator spell later today and give the results to Mallory tomorrow. Then it will be a simple matter of visiting up the cursed person, telling them that they're a werewolf, if they don't already know, and locking them away with Timothy when there's a full moon."

"You want me to visit them while you're away?" Mallory asked.

"No, wait until we get back. We have plenty of time. You could look around for a place to lock them up, though. Preferably somewhere remote."

"Sure, will do."

"I guess we should head to the lake," I told Felicity. "Do you have a bag you're taking?"

"There's a suitcase in my office."

"Okay, I'll grab it on the way out." I handed Mallory my office key and house key, noticing a look of disapproval on Felicity's face as I did so. "Lock up when you leave the office. I'd tell you to help yourself to anything in the house but there's nothing there, so you're going to have to stock the fridge yourself." I grinned at her.

"Ah, so this is all just a ploy to make me go grocery shopping for you," she said.

"Yeah, and feel free to unpack all those boxes in the house, too."

She gave me an amused look. "You guys have a great time at the lake while I do all the hard work."

"Okay," I said, kissing her forehead lightly before leaving the office. "We will. See ya later."

I got Felicity's case, a weekend-sized pale blue hard-shelled job, from her office and took it down the stairs. Felicity followed without a word until we reached the Land Rover and I was hefting her case into the back. "Are you sure it's okay to give Mallory the keys to the office and your house?"

"Yeah, of course it is. She's a good friend. I trust her."

"All right," she said, climbing into the passenger seat. "As long as you're sure."

"I'm very sure. Mallory and I are close. There's a bond between us."

"Yes, I can tell that by the way you are with each other," she said flatly. After picking up the GPS from the floor, she programed it and attached it to the windshield.

I wasn't sure how she had meant to convey that last statement. Her voice had been devoid of any inflection but almost as if she were trying to hide some emotion behind the words. Was she resentful of my relationship with Mallory? Maybe she was just sad that she was so far from her boyfriend and seeing Mallory and me rubbed it in. Not that there was anything between Mallory and I other than a weird physical therapy that was probably damaging to both of us, but I could understand how our easy interactions with each other might be seen by an outsider.

If I was a sensitive kind of guy, I'd probably just ignore Felicity's remark, putting it down to the fact that she had some sort of problem in her personal life and probably didn't want to talk about it. I'd keep quiet and let her tell me in her own time.

But instead of doing that, as I backed out of the parking space, I asked, "How's Jason?"

She eyed me suspiciously. "What do you mean?"

"Jason. Your boyfriend. You left the barbecue early because he was going to call you."

"He's fine."

I joined the light traffic on Main Street. "What does he do? For a living, I mean."

"He's an accountant for a bank in London."

That was a conversation stopper. Jason sounded dependable and boring. I couldn't think of anything else to say, so I just said, "Cool," and focused on driving.

A while later, after we had left Dearmont and were driving north along the highway, Felicity said, "He's not very happy about me being here."

"Hmm?" Her sudden openness after almost an hour of quiet took me by surprise. I'd been dwelling on the fact that there might be a false memory implanted in my mind, replacing a real memory that was locked behind a magical door, according to Devon Blackwell.

"Jason," Felicity said. "He doesn't like me being over here while he's over there in England. I knew he wasn't happy about it when I told him about the job in the first place, but he didn't say anything, apart from being sulky whenever I spoke about it. Perhaps he thought I wouldn't actually go through with it and move here. Last night, he asked me to go back to England."

"Oh. What did you tell him?"

"I told him that my career is important to me and that I'll be staying here."

Even though I barely knew Felicity, I was glad to hear that she wasn't tempted to fly back to England. "I guess he wasn't too happy to hear that."

"No, he wasn't. He told me...." She hesitated, her breath hitching a little as if she were trying to hold back tears. "He told me I have to make a decision. My career or him."

"Oh, I'm sorry to hear that," I said. I actually thought that Jason sounded like a giant douchebag and Felicity was better off without him, but I didn't say that, of course.

She nodded in acknowledgement but didn't say anything. Instead, she folded her arms and sank further into her seat, as if withdrawing from the world.

I went back to thinking about magical locked doors and enchantments that could alter memories.

CHAPTER 13

IT WAS LATE AFTERNOON BY the time we reached Dark Rock Lake. A narrow, bumpy access road led us deep into the trees to the area where the cabins sat by a small beach. The lake was surrounded on all sides by dense forest. The beach was busy with vacationing families and couples, which was very different to how it had been when James and his friends had been here in April. Children ran by the lake's edge, screaming and laughing while their parents watched from picnic tables in the shade. As well as the cabins, there were RVs parked beneath the pine trees.

As I parked the Land Rover and killed the engine, Felicity looked at the trees all around us "How are we going to find the entrance to Faerie? There are miles of forest to search. It could take forever."

"If we were searching by conventional means," I said. "I brought something along that's going to make it a little easier than that."

"Something magical?"

"Yeah, it's a magical statue."

"So let's get it and start searching," she suggested.

"It isn't that simple. We can't go wandering through the woods with a magical item, looking for a doorway to Faerie, while there are all these people around. We need to be more discreet. If there are this many people on the beach, there'll be just as many on the hiking trails. Besides, the statue only works at twilight."

"Oh, okay. So we're stuck here for a while." She turned in her seat to face me. "Can I ask you a question? You got the witches to cast a locator spell to find the werewolf in town, so why not ask them to cast a locator spell to find James and Sarah?"

"A locator spell can't locate something that isn't there. James and Sarah are in a different realm of existence. A locator spell only works in the realm in which it's cast, so a spell cast here can't locate someone in Faerie." I opened my door. "Let's get our stuff into the cabin. I need to stretch my legs after that long drive." I got out of the Land Rover and walked around to the back. There was a strong tang of pinewood in the air, along with an underlying smell of burning charcoal from the barbecues outside the cabins and RVs.

Felicity and I got our luggage and found Cabin No. 6, the one we had rented for the next three days. The key to the cabin was locked inside a metal safe attached to the outside wall. Felicity punched in the code she had been given and opened the safe to retrieve the key. She opened the door and we went inside.

The cabin was basic but clean and tidy. There was a living area, a small kitchen, and a short corridor that led to two bedrooms and a bathroom. I claimed the bedroom that looked out over the parking area, letting Felicity take the one that overlooked the beach. After all, if I found the entrance to Faerie tonight, I might not be sleeping in the cabin at all. Because of the time dilation between the two realms, I would go to search for James and Sarah for a couple of hours and when I got back, a couple of days might have passed here. It might be time to head back to Dearmont as soon as I returned from the faerie realm. And if I had James and Sarah with me, they would want to get home as soon as possible.

When I got back to the kitchen Felicity was making coffee. "Not for me, thanks," I told her. "I won't be eating anything either."

"Why not?" she asked, pouring coffee into a mug for herself.

"Faerie is a dangerous place and there's lore that says a traveler should be fasted and purified before attempting to go there. A couple of centuries ago, people would fast for days before going to Faerie to protect them from the beings there. I don't have that luxury, and I think those people may have been overcautious, but I can at least skip a meal and a coffee before I face the faerie folk in their own realm."

"Should I be worried about you?"

"Traveling to Faerie is dangerous," I said. "There's a long history of people getting trapped there and being unable to return to our world. But as long as I keep my wits about me, I'll be fine. You don't have to worry unless I'm gone for a long time, but it's difficult to know how long because of the way time works differently between here and Faerie. If it's more than a week, inform the Society. They'll probably send a rescue party to get me back."

"A week?" Felicity looked shocked.

"Like I said, it should only be a couple of days our time. If it's a week, I'm probably stuck there."

"All right," she said, bringing her coffee to the sofa and sitting down. She looked a little overwhelmed. Maybe she wished she'd gone back to boring douchebag Jason and taken up accountancy instead of having to deal with the possibility of her boss being lost in the faerie realm.

"Felicity, don't worry about me. I've been to Faerie, and come back alive and well, many times."

"How many?"

I didn't have to search very far into my memory to find the answer to that question. "Once," I admitted.

"Once?" She nearly spat out her coffee. "You've only done this once before?"

"Once is better than never."

"Alec, maybe this isn't such a good idea. There must be another way. What if we go to the Robinson house and confront the faerie that's pretending to be him? You could kill it. And do the same with the one pretending to be Sarah."

"Those two kids will still be trapped in Faerie," I said. "The only way they're coming back is if I go there and rescue them."

She went quiet after that, probably deciding that I was about to embark on a suicide mission.

She drank some more of her coffee while I stood by the window, watching the people on the beach. Those people didn't ever worry about preternatural beings trying to kill them, or werewolves prowling on the night of the full moon.

In a way, I envied them that innocence. I'd been thrust into the world of the preternatural at a young age by a father determined that I should follow in his footsteps as a member of the Society of Shadows. My mom had rebelled, telling my father that I should live a normal childhood, eventually leaving him and taking me to Oregon, the place of her birth, where she and I had family.

For a few years, I'd grown up like any other kid and been concerned only with the usual, mundane things that trouble a boy of ten. But two days after my tenth birthday, that all changed. My mother was killed in a car accident and my father, upon hearing the news, came to Oregon to claim me and return me to an education at the Academy of Shadows in England. That education included training in preternatural investigation, the history of the Society of Shadows, hand-to-hand combat, and the use of weapons.

Most of the people out there on the beach at Dark Rock Lake would call my upbringing "cool" or "awesome" but they all possessed something that I could never have: an assurance that the things they saw in horror movies were fake. That monsters didn't really exist and nothing lurked in the shadows.

I could never have that assurance. I knew that the boogeyman did exist and the shadows were crawling with horrors. And knowing those things, I felt a responsibility to protect others from them.

That was why, when innocent people were taken from their mundane existence and thrown headfirst into the world of the preternatural, I felt duty-bound to fight the shadows and return the victims to their normal lives. I couldn't turn my back on James Robinson and Sarah Silverman, even if it meant risking everything.

From behind me, Felicity said, "Okay, how are we going to find the door into Faerie?"

I went to the bedroom and opened my sports bag, removing the item I'd brought from home. It was wrapped in a plain white cloth and was the same size as Felicity's coffee mug, although it weighed a lot more. When I put it on the coffee table, Felicity leaned forward and asked, "What is it?"

I pulled the cloth away, revealing a crude stone bust of a two-headed, bearded man. The two heads faced in opposite directions, joined at the back. "This is a statue of Janus," I said. "He was an ancient Roman god of doorways, gates, and time. There are plenty of statues of Janus around, but this one is enchanted. Once activated, it leads the user to magical doorways that are in the area."

She reached out to touch the stone bust. "Can I?" she asked, her hand hesitating, inches away.

"Sure, go ahead. Until it's activated, it's nothing more than a piece of rock."

She stroked its carved surface. "If it has two heads facing opposite ways, how do you know which head is pointing at the doorway you want to find? I assume that's how it works, by pointing in the direction you want to go."

"Yeah, there's some interpretation involved," I said. "You have to make a guess as to which head is pointing in the right direction. Sometimes it's easy, like if one head was pointing at the forest and other at the lake, we'd know to go into the forest. But sometimes, you don't know which head to follow. It takes some trial and error and doubling back. It's magic, not science."

"So it could take us some time to find the entrance to Faerie."

"Yeah, and we can't start looking until twilight. That's the only time the Janus statue works, because twilight is what's called an 'in-between' time, between night and day, and doorways are portals between things."

Felicity went to the kitchen to pour herself another coffee. "So we wait."

"Yeah, we wait." I looked up at the late afternoon sky. It wouldn't be long now.

* * *

When twilight arrived, I went to the Land Rover to get my sword. The sky had turned a deep, dark blue, stained with patches of purple. The beach was much quieter, most of the families sitting around fires and barbecues eating supper. The savory smell of burgers, hot dogs, and grilled fish made my stomach growl.

I took the sword, hidden beneath its cloth wrapping, back to the cabin where Felicity waited with the Janus statue in her hands. "You ready?" I asked her.

"Yeah, let's do it."

Before we left the cabin, I recited the Latin words that activated the statue and were inscribed on its base. There was no visible change in the statue's appearance—it didn't glow or anything—but Felicity said, "Oh, it's pulling against my grip."

"Hold it very loosely," I told her. "Cup it gently so it can rotate."

She did, holding the statue in front of her, cupped in both hands. Slowly, Janus rotated so that one head looked out toward the lake and the other pointed toward the back of the cabin and the forest.

"I told you the first part would be easy," I said.

We left the cabin and went into the forest, finding a hiking trail that went in the general direction the statue was pointing. I carried my sword, still wrapped, in one hand. If anyone passed us on the trail, they might think I was carrying fishing gear. Hopefully, they wouldn't wonder why I was carrying it away from the lake.

"Stop here," I said. "Check Janus." The statue had shifted slightly in Felicity's grip but I wasn't sure if that was because she was holding it too tightly.

She held it up and relaxed her grip. Janus continued to point along the trail, and since the opposing head pointed back the way we had come, I was pretty sure we were headed in the right direction. It made sense. Leon Smith had said that James and Sarah were daring each other to come into the woods, neither of them really wanting to, so they probably didn't venture far and would have stayed on the trail. Assuming the faeries that abducted them stayed close to the doorway to Faerie, the portal shouldn't be too far from here.

We walked on for a few hundred yards before I heard a sound that made my senses go into overdrive. I tapped Felicity on the shoulder and put my finger to my lips. She nodded and froze in place.

The forest was gloomy now, the spaces beneath the trees hidden by dark shadows. I heard the noise again;

footfalls on the trail behind us. "We're being followed," I whispered to Felicity. Her eyes widened with fear, staring into the darkness on our back trail.

"Maybe it's just someone taking a walk," she suggested.

"No, they're trying not to be heard."

"How many of them are there?"

"Two. One large, one smaller."

I unwrapped the sword, tossed the cloth to the ground and moved into a fighting stance, facing the source of the footfalls. The enchanted blade glowed vivid blue, lighting up the trees around me, chasing away the shadows.

The footfalls halted. Whoever was back there had seen the blue light ahead of them on the trail. After a moment, the footfalls resumed, slower this time, hesitant. Hell, maybe Felicity had been right and it was just a couple taking a romantic walk through the woods. Just as I was wondering how I was going to explain away the fact that I was standing in the middle of the trail holding a glowing blue sword, two familiar faces appeared out of the darkness. When I saw who it was, I lowered my weapon.

"Leon, what the hell are you doing here?"

Leon Smith came up to us with a sheepish look on his face. He was wearing a black sweater, black jeans, and black boots, and had a black knitted beanie perched on his head. He looked like he might have stepped out of a Mission Impossible movie.

Similarly attired, and standing behind Leon, was his butler Michael. Clutched in Michael's hands, its barrel pointing over his left shoulder, was a shotgun.

"Hey," Leon said. "What are you guys doing out here?"

"I just asked you the same question. And why is Michael carrying that gun?"

"Why are you carrying that sword?" He looked at the weapon with wide eyes, the blue glow illuminating his face. "That thing is sweet."

"Leon," I repeated, "what are you doing here?"

"After you guys came by yesterday, I decided to do some investigating of my own, so I bought an RV and came up here to take a look around. Of course, I had no idea what I was looking for until you showed up this afternoon. So I waited to see where you were going and followed you."

"Go back," I said. "This is no place for you."

"Because it's supernatural, right?"

I nodded. "Yes."

"Sign me up. It's about time something excited happened in my life. You know, living in a huge mansion and being able to buy anything you want isn't all it's cracked up to be. I'm bored, man. When you guys visited me yesterday, it was the most exciting thing that's happened in my life in a long time. So I'm here to help. Can I get a sword like that one?"

"No," I said, losing my patience. "Leon, this isn't a game. Go back to your RV."

"You're out here trying to find out what happened to James, right?" he asked.

I nodded.

"Well James was my best friend," he said. "Before he changed, we used to hang out together all the time. Since he came into these woods, that all went to shit. I want to know what happened to my friend, and I'm not going to just walk away from this."

I sighed, unsure of what to do next. Twilight was running out fast and once it did, the Janus statue wouldn't work anymore. "We're looking for something," I said, "and we need to find it before twilight ends, so I don't have time to argue with you. Please, for your own good, leave it to us to help your friend."

"Whatever you're looking for, we can help," he said.

"Fine. If you're not going to go back, you can come with us. But once we find what we're looking for, you and Michael will stay here with Felicity. Do not try to follow me."

"Sure," Leon said, nodding enthusiastically. "So are we looking for a cave or something?"

"New rule," I said. "Keep quiet. Felicity, check Janus."

She held up the statue. One face still looked at the path ahead of us.

"Let's go," I said. We set off along the path, Felicity in the lead, Leon and I following, and Michael bringing up the rear.

"So, are you going to tell me what's happening?" Leon asked. "Why are we following a statue of a two-headed dude?"

I thought back to when we'd interviewed Leon at his house. He hadn't seemed worried that we were preternatural investigators; in fact, he'd seemed excited by the idea. Some people were able to handle the supernatural better than others, usually depending on their upbringing and beliefs. Maybe Leon would be able to handle the truth.

"Have you had any experience of the supernatural?" I asked him.

"Not directly, but my grandma was into all that stuff. She used to tell me stories when I was a kid that were like fairy tales but, like, ten times more gory. And her neighbors used to come see her when they needed healing potions or a spell to get rid of a curse, stuff like that. She used to brew all kinds of weird concoctions in her kitchen and her place always smelled like herbs and flowers. I loved visiting her house."

"She ever tell you about faeries?"

"Yeah, she believed in all that."

"Felicity, check Janus," I said. She held up the statue and it twisted in her hand so that the heads pointed away from the trail. One face looked left, the other right. Shit. This was where the ambiguous nature of the statue's magic could get us lost.

"Which way?" Felicity asked.

All I could see in both directions was darkness and trees. "Left," I said. "If we don't find anything after a couple of minutes and the faces are still pointing in the same direction, we'll come back to the trail and go the other way."

We stepped off the trail and made our way through the undergrowth, twigs snapping and leaves crackling beneath our boots.

"You think there are faeries in these woods?" Leon asked me in a whisper. His eyes scanned the darkness beyond the glow of my sword.

"Did your grandma ever tell you that faeries sometimes trap humans in their realm, a place known as Faerie?"

"Yeah," he said. "That's their basic trick, isn't it?"

"You could say that." I silently thanked Leon's grandmother for giving her grandson an understanding of the preternatural world. It made what I was about to say easier. "That's what I think happened to James and Sarah."

"They were taken by faeries? But we saw them. They went home."

"What you saw were two faeries pretending to be James and Sarah."

He went quiet, letting that sink in for a moment. Then he whispered, "Holy fuck."

"I'm going to get them back," I said.

Felicity stopped and pointed into the trees. "Alec, is that it? Janus is pointing right at it."

I followed the direction of her pointing finger, using the sword's enchanted blue glow to illuminate the area. We had come to a rocky bluff and in the face of the rock, a narrow cave entrance stretched up from the ground to the height of my head. I knew that faerie doorways were usually situated at the same locations of doorways and portals in our realm, so this was probably the place. There was only one way to find out.

"Felicity, put Janus on the ground in the cave entrance, one head facing inside, the other facing out." She did as I asked and the cave entrance began to glow with a pale green luminescence. Beyond the glow, instead of the dark interior of the cave, I could see another forest, this one lit by sunlight. The Janus statue had opened the door to Faerie.

I went over to Felicity and said, "Listen carefully. Come here at twilight, before dawn and before nightfall, every day, and put the Janus statue in that exact place and position to open the doorway for me. There are many ways in and out of Faerie, but at least I'll know that this way is open if I can't find another way out."

She nodded. "I'll do it exactly as you said. Please be careful. Safe journey." She raised her head and kissed my cheek.

"I'll be fine," I assured her with a smile. I turned to tell Leon that I was going to bring his friend back alive and well, but he wasn't there. "Where's Leon?" I asked

Michael, already feeling a cold dread at the pit of my stomach.

He nodded at the glowing open doorway to Faerie. "He said he was going to find his friend, sir, and he went through the portal."

The portal flickered for a moment, as if it were unstable. Twilight was ending and the night was about to fall. When that happened, the Janus statue would stop working and the portal would close until the next twilight before dawn.

There was no time for hesitation. I stepped through the portal and into Faerie.

CHAPTER 14

TEN SECONDS AFTER I STEPPED through the portal, it vanished. I was standing in front of a cave entrance similar to the one in my own realm, but there was no pale green glow or a vision of my own world beyond, simply a dark fissure in the rock face.

The day was bright, the forest seemingly alive with birds singing and small woodland creatures that I couldn't see, but could hear moving about in the undergrowth. There was a sweet smell of wildflowers hanging in the air that was so strong it was intoxicating.

That was the problem with Faerie; everything here was intoxicating to humans, making us want to stay here forever. There were strict rules for visiting Faerie and getting out again, and the golden rule was not to eat or drink anything here. If you did that, you might as well kiss goodbye to any thoughts of going home, because it was never going to happen.

I looked on the ground for tracks that Leon might have left, telling me which direction he'd taken, but the grass and roots looked undisturbed. At least I had a general idea of which way he'd gone, because behind me was the rock face. He definitely hadn't gone that way, so I strode forward, keeping my vision sharp and the sword tightly gripped in my hand.

Leon couldn't have gone far; I'd arrived through the portal a few seconds after he had. I called his name, the sound of my voice making the birds and animals halt their song and movement. The forest became silent.

There was no answer from Leon. He couldn't be out of earshot already, but for some reason, he wasn't responding to my voice. That was bad. I quickened my pace, striding through the forest as fast as I could while still looking for any kind of trail Leon might have left. But I saw no broken branches on the trees or snapped twigs on the ground where he might have stepped. The undergrowth seemed undisturbed. I turned around and checked the area behind me. There was no evidence that I had passed this way. It was as if the forest were closing behind me. It was too damned easy to get lost here.

Ahead, I saw a clearing, and I could hear the song-like tinkling of running water. I could also see Leon, his back to me, looking down at something in front of him. "Leon!" I shouted, running toward him.

He didn't turn around. He didn't move at all.

The trees gave way to the clearing, where a rocky pool glistened in the sunlight. Frolicking in the shimmering water were two naked female faeries. They had long blonde hair that clung to the tempting curves of their bodies and spread out along the surface of the pool. Their eyes were completely pale blue with no white at all. Despite their otherworldly appearance, or maybe because of it, the faerie women were stunning, exotic creatures and their appearance caused my mind to imagine sexual scenarios involving them and me. But they didn't only stimulate my sex drive; my heart ached as I looked at their beauty.

I knew now why Leon was standing there staring at the women in the pool. What else was there to do? What possible purpose in life could have a man have other than to gaze upon such wonderful creatures? I approached the pool, my eyes fixed on the two faerie women as they swam and played in the silvery water. When I reached Leon, I looked at him and said, "I wondered why you didn't reply to my call, but now I know."

He nodded slowly, his gaze following the occupants of the pool as they swam in sensuous circles. "Yeah, I just want to look at them forever."

So did I. The pattern of their movements seemed to speak to some deep part of my mind, as if their perfect bodies were describing symbols of some forgotten language that a primal part of my being recognized from aeons past. It was mesmerizing.

A sudden burning sensation along my ribs made me grimace with pain and brought me to my senses. My head cleared, as if a strong wind had blown away a dense fog that was obscuring my thoughts. I pulled up my shirt, seeking the source of the pain in my side, and found that one of my protection tattoos was glowing an angry red. As I felt the glamor I had been under vanish, the tattoo returned to its normal black color.

What the hell had I been thinking, standing here watching the faeries in the pool? I knew how easy it was to be trapped in this enticing realm yet I'd fallen for it hook, line, and sinker. I had to be more careful; the tattoos couldn't protect me from every type of magic or glamor.

I grabbed Leon's shoulders and shook them. "Hey, Leon, look away. Come on, we're leaving here."

He continued to stare at the faeries in the pool. I had to physically drag him away and even then, he fought against me to go back to the water's edge. I slapped him across the face hard, wondering if that might snap him out of it. It didn't. He kept fighting against me, but me was only half-hearted about it because his attention was focused on the pool.

It wasn't until I dragged him into the trees, out of sight of the clearing, that he regained his senses. "What happened?" he asked. "I was looking at those women in the pool."

"You were under a glamor," I told him. "This place is dangerous, which is why I told you to stay away."

He shrugged. "I just want to help James."

"I can't do anything about the fact that you're here now," I said. "But listen closely to what I tell you. Stay close to me at all times. Don't eat or drink anything. If anyone offers you anything ... food, drink, sex ... refuse. Don't even think about it, just say no. And if anyone wants to make a bargain with you, even one that sounds great, say no."

"Sex?" he asked.

I rolled my eyes. "The faeries will do anything to trap you here. Sex is the oldest trick in their book. Look, just stick close to me and refuse anything and everything that is offered to you."

"Okay, man." He looked at the forest around us. "How the hell are we going to find James here? It's all just trees and more trees."

I dug into my pocket and pulled out a silver Saint Anthony medallion. "We're going to use this." I held it up to show him. "Saint Anthony is the patron saint of lost things and people."

He arched an eyebrow. "Dude, that's Catholic. You use that stuff as well as Janus and all that?"

"I use whatever works. I've found missing people with this before. It was blessed by seven Catholic priests in Ireland in the seventeenth century. I'd have used it to find you if I hadn't seen you at the pool." I recited the prayer that activated the medallion and added James's name at the end. If he was in this area, the medallion would lead us to him.

But the medallion did nothing. It hung from its chain and did not move.

"What does that mean?" Leon asked.

"I don't know. It usually moves, pointing the way to the lost person."

"Try it again."

I recited the prayer again, this time saying Sarah's name. The result was the same. The medallion didn't move.

"Do you think it means they're dead?" James asked, a worried look passing across his face.

"No, I'm sure it doesn't mean that."

"But if that thing can't pick up their life force or whatever, maybe it's because they're dead."

"They're not dead," I assured him. "Faeries don't kill their victims; they trap them here. Unless...." I felt a sinking feeling in the pit of my stomach. Maybe I was looking at this all wrong. I had assumed that a couple of faeries had gone through the portal from here to our realm, lured James and Sarah here, and used a glamor to assume their identities. That was the usual way faeries took on the guise of humans, but there was another, more sinister, way that was the *modus operandi* of a much darker faerie being.

"Leon, when I asked you if there was a full moon that night at the lake, you said there wasn't. You said you couldn't remember any moon in the night sky, is that right?"

"Yeah, that's right, there were stars but no moon."

At the time, I had thought that there might be a new moon, the phase of the moon when it appears totally black. I should have followed that train of thought, because the new moon might have been a clue to what actually happened to James and Sarah.

"And James and Sarah brought something back from the woods with them. Something heavy."

"Yeah, man, whatever they found that turned them crazy."

"No, it wasn't that," I said. "It wasn't that at all. We need to get back home. James and Sarah are in even more danger than I thought."

Leon was looking at something behind me. "They're not the only ones."

I turned to face two faerie warriors. They were tall and slender, wearing bone and leather armor. They each held a long spear tipped with a deadly-looking stone point that was pointed at us. Their features and bearing were beautiful but their manner was hostile. "What are you doing in this forest, human?" one of them asked me. His voice was light and airy, but it held a menace in its tone.

"We're leaving," I said. "Right now."

The other faerie shook his head, the bone and bead decorations in his long hair rattling as he did so. "You are coming with us. The Lady of the Forest will decide what to do with you."

I lifted the sword in my hand slightly. "Look, I don't want to hurt anyone. Like I said, we're leaving."

"You are not leaving," the warrior closest to me said, jabbing my shirt with the point of his spear. It looked like I was going to have to fight my way out of here. I tightened my grip on the hilt of the sword and prepared to attack.

"What is going on here?" said a soft, feminine voice from my left. I turned my head that way to see a long-legged female faerie seated on a wooden throne carved with intricate knot designs and bird and animal motifs. She wore a circlet of ivy leaves around her head and had brightly-colored flowers decorating her long blonde hair. Her clothing was a simple white dress that clung diaphanously to her bountiful figure. The throne upon which she sat was mounted on wooden cross bars and being carried by humans wearing brown tunics and vine collars around their necks.

Escorting the throne were at least a dozen warriors in armor similar to the two scouts who had found Leon and me.

The faerie who had prodded my chest with his spear bowed slightly to the throne. "Humans, my lady. We found them wandering the forest."

She turned her ice blue eyes toward me. "What are you doing here, mortal?"

I sighed. This was obviously the Lady of the Forest and we were in her territory. Getting out of here wasn't going to be as easy as I'd thought.

CHAPTER 15

THE LADY OF THE FOREST gestured to us with one slender hand. "Bring them to me."

The scouts led us at spear-point to the throne.

"Your names?" the Lady asked us.

"Leon, ma'am," Leon said in a low voice. "Leon Smith."

"Alec Harbinger, P.I.," I said levelly. I knew that our best chance to get out of here in one piece was to not show any weakness that the faeries could exploit.

"P.I.?" she asked. Her voice was soft and low and her words seemed to melt into my mind.

"Preternatural Investigator."

She frowned momentarily. "You work for that wretched society. What are you doing in my forest?"

"We weren't aware that this was your forest, my lady," I said, knowing how much faeries loved custom and societal niceties, "otherwise we would have sought you out to inform you of our visit. As I was telling your soldier, we were just about to leave here and return to our own realm."

"I will ask you one more time, Alec Harbinger. Why are you here?"

"We were looking for two friends of ours, thinking that they might be in this realm, but now I know that they aren't."

"More humans?"

I nodded.

"Apart from my slaves," she said, indicating the throne-bearers, "there have not been any humans in this part of Faerie for quite a while. Why did you believe you would find them here in my forest?"

"I thought they had been trapped here while two faeries took their place in the human world. I now know that isn't true. They've been in the human world the entire time."

"Intriguing," she said, leaning forward, her flower hair decorations blooming slightly. "Tell me of this human drama."

I told her what I had recently figured out. "Our friends were taken by changelings."

Her face screwed up, but it was still pretty. "Ugh, those vile creatures." She turned to one of the warriors, a faerie who wore a thick armband of bones on his left arm. "I thought those things had been banished from my forest."

"Yes, my lady, they were," he said with a bow of his head. "What the human is talking about happened in the human world after we banished them."

The Lady of the Forest looked at me again. "I want nothing to do with those disgusting monsters."

"Then we'll be on our way," I suggested, hoping that her revulsion at the changelings that had once lived in this forest would make her want to let us leave. If we reminded her of something that was abhorrent to her, wasn't it better for her to just let us go and forget about us?

"You know it isn't that simple, mortal," she said. "I require an exchange."

I groaned inwardly. This was exactly what I'd been hoping to avoid. But now I knew that James and Sarah had been taken by changelings, I also knew that the clock was ticking before they were killed and the changelings assumed their identities permanently. I didn't have time to haggle with the Lady of the Forest, but I couldn't just agree to anything. Faeries knew when they had an advantage and they loved to exploit it.

"What sort of exchange?" I asked her.

"Don't sound so downtrodden," she said lightly. "Is it really so bad to strike a bargain with the Lady of the Forest? Maybe I can think of something that is beneficial to both of us. Tell me what you want, Alec, and you can have it."

"I want to get out of here."

A smile lit her face. "Something so simple?"

"Yes, a simple thing that won't require much in return."

The Lady of the Forest pouted slightly. "You're taking all the fun out of it. Let me think what would be a suitable exchange for safe passage out of Faerie."

"We don't need safe passage," I said. "Just show us the door and we're gone." I wanted to keep my end of the deal as basic as possible so she couldn't ask too much in return. She would suggest an escort of armed faerie guards all the way back to our world and then from Dark Rock Lake to Dearmont if she thought it meant she could ask for more from me in the exchange.

"Very well. In exchange for what you ask, I will require a simple thing in return. At some time in the future, I may require your services. I shall send an envoy to you in your world and ask that you do something for me."

"Do what?" I asked. I wasn't going to agree to something so vague.

"I don't know yet. I'm sure a man of your talents may be needed to aid the Lady of the Forest in some way."

"No deal. I'm not agreeing to anything unless I know exactly what it is."

She sighed. "All right. When my envoy informs you of the task required, you may refuse. But until you accept a task, you will be in my debt."

"And I get told what the task is before I accept or refuse?"

"Of course. I can see you're no fun. There's no daring in your spirit. You will be told the tasks and you decide whether to accept or not upon hearing their nature."

It sounded fair. I could refuse tasks until I was offered one that was simple and safe. Although "safe" was a relative word when dealing with faeries.

"And you show us the way back to our own world immediately," I said.

"Yes, of course. I'm already bored with you."

"I accept." As soon as I said the words, I felt a rush of energy rise from the ground up through my feet. It spread up my body like a warm tingle, snaking up my spine until it reached my head. I felt dizzy for a few seconds but then it passed and I felt refreshed, as if I'd just had a relaxing sleep. A new flower, a white lily, bloomed in the Lady of the Forest's hair. Whether I liked it or not, she and I were now bonded until I paid my debt to her.

To keep her side of the bargain, she stood and faced the forest on the right side of her throne before waving her right hand in a delicate pattern in the air in front of her. A pale green glow appeared, and beyond it, I could see the faery forest's equivalent in my own world. I grabbed Leon's arm and led him to the portal.

Without a word to the faeries, we stepped through and found ourselves in a pine forest that I was sure was the same one we had left earlier to travel to Faerie. But how much earlier? I took my phone out of my pocket to check the date and the GPS, but the damn thing was trying to sync. Traveling to other realms wasn't part of my cellphone plan.

So I had no idea what day it was or exactly where we were. It was daytime—afternoon, judging by the position of the sun where I could see it through the gaps in the towering pines—and it was warm and humid.

"Do you hear that?" Leon asked me. He cocked his head, listening for something.

I heard it too. The sound of children laughing. "It's this way," I said, trudging through the undergrowth.

We found a trail and followed it down a slight incline. When we reached the bottom, we could see the beach and the cabins through the trees. At least the Lady of the Forest had opened a doorway near our destination.

As we walked toward the cabins, I could tell we'd been gone for some time. The cars in the parking lot weren't the same ones that had been there when we'd entered the woods at twilight with the Janus statue. I was glad to see the Land Rover there, but it was parked in a different location. Maybe Felicity had needed to use it for some reason. I opened the back and put my sword inside, out of the way.

We reached Cabin No. 6 and I tried the door. It was locked, so I knocked. A large tattooed man opened it. "Yeah?"

I hesitated, confused. "I'm looking for Felicity. She's a tall, English woman with long, dark hair and glasses. Have you seen her?"

He looked at me as if I was crazy. "Wrong cabin, Pal," he said as he closed the door in my face.

Felicity had rented the cabin for three days. Surely we hadn't been gone for longer than that.

"Come on, man, let's go to my RV," Leon said. "Michael will let us know what's been happening since we've been gone."

I followed him to a large, new RV. He banged on the door. "Michael, you in there?"

The door opened immediately and Michael, who had looked worried when he opened the door, grinned. "Sir, you're back."

"Yes, now let us in." He climbed the steps into the RV and I followed. The interior still had that brand-new vehicle smell. Judging by the white leather seats and expensive looking everything, this RV was definitely at the higher end of the market.

Felicity was sitting at the table in the living area. When she saw me, her face lit up. "Alec!"

"Okay, listen up," I said, sliding in behind the table next to her and gesturing Leon and Michael over. "I was wrong about James and Sarah. They weren't taken to Faerie. They were attacked in the woods by creatures known as changelings. Now, unlike other faeries, who trap their victims in Faerie and use a glamor to look like them, changelings slowly transform into a physical copy of their victim. It takes a while and they need to feed off the original body every night.

"That's why you heard them dragging something heavy back from the woods and why they wouldn't let anyone into their cabin," I told Leon. "They didn't find anything in the woods; they were bringing James and Sarah's bodies back to feed off them. When they left the lake the day after you, they must have taken the bodies with them. During the transformation, the changeling can't be too far from the victim's body. That's why James won't leave the house."

"And he's going into the woods every night to feed from the body?" Felicity asked. "That's gross."

I nodded. "They probably have the bodies hidden in that little graveyard. Sarah's house is on the other side of those woods, so that would be an ideal location for them both to go at night and feed. Also, when we were there, I saw hawthorn vines growing there. Hawthorn grows in places where there's magical energy. James and Sarah will be in an enchanted sleep. It's a magical sleep that keeps them in a kind of suspended animation."

"Like in the fairy tales," Leon said. "Snow White and Sleeping Beauty and all that."

"Exactly like that," I said. "And they'll be like that for three full moons. The changeling attacks its victim on a new moon because the new moon symbolizes new beginnings, and for the changeling, the transformation is a new beginning. Then it feeds every night until the third full moon, when it rips out the sleeping victim's heart and changes permanently into a copy of that person."

I looked at Felicity. "The full moon that is approaching will be the third full moon after James and Sarah were attacked at the lake. So we need to stop the changelings by the next full moon or it'll be too late. They'll rip out James and Sarah's hearts and complete the transformation."

The color drained from Felicity's face. "Alec, you've been gone for five days. The full moon is tonight."

CHAPTER 16

I CAN'T BELIEVE IT WAS five days," I said as we sped along the highway. Felicity was driving the Land Rover and I was in the passenger seat so I could call Mallory as soon as there was a signal on the phone. Leon and Michael were following us in the RV.

Mallory was going to have to deal with Timothy and the other werewolf tonight while I dealt with the changelings. James and Sarah would die tonight if I didn't find their bodies and wake them up. The changelings would assume their identities forever. Now it made sense why Changeling James had been asking Amelia Robinson about her will. Changelings loved treasure and there was probably no better treasure than controlling interest in a huge lumber company. It seemed like faeries were becoming modernized. Once, treasure meant a pot of gold coins; now it was stocks and shares.

I shook my phone as if that would somehow make a signal appear. "Is your phone working?" I asked Felicity.

"It's in my handbag by your feet."

I got her phone and checked it. No signal.

"Alec," Felicity said, "there's something I need to tell you."

"Okay, what is it?"

"When you didn't come back from Faerie for five days, I rang the Society."

"What? Why? I told you not to."

She bit her lip. "You said you'd be gone for two or three days and to call the Society if you were gone for a week."

"Yes, but I wasn't gone for a week."

"You said a couple of days, so when it stretched out to five, I became worried."

Great. So now I also had to call the Society to tell them to cancel the rescue party, if there'd ever been one in the first place. But first I had to call Mallory. She had to deal with those werewolves.

My phone buzzed a few times. I looked at the screen. I had texts from Mallory asking where I was. More importantly, I had a signal. I called Mallory.

"Alec, where the hell are you? It's been...."

"Five days, yes, I know. The time dilation between here and Faerie was a little different to what I expected."

"Did you find James and Sarah?"

"No, they're not in Faerie. I think they're hidden in a small family graveyard on the Robinson estate."

"Are they alive?"

"They won't be if we don't get to them tonight."

"No problem. Count me in."

"It isn't as simple as that. We need to lock up the werewolves, too. Did you find out who the other werewolf is?"

"Yeah, it's a girl named Josie Carter. She lives with her mother on the opposite side of town to Timothy. I drove by her place a couple of times but I didn't make contact with her, just as you asked. Of course, if I didn't hear from you in the next couple of hours, I would have had to go talk with her."

"Sorry about that. Did you find a place to lock them away for the night?"

"Yeah, there's an old abandoned place south of town called McDermott's Farm. I broke in and checked it out. There's a basement with a sturdy door. Should be perfect."

"Okay, you get Timothy and Josie over there while I head over to the Robinson place. I'll meet you at the farm after I wake James and Sarah from an enchanted sleep and kill the changelings."

"Sounds like I get the easy job this time," Mallory said.

"You mean like most times." Before she could answer, I ended the call.

My next call was to Blackwell Books. Victoria answered and I asked her if she had the ingredients to make a foxglove paste.

"I do," she said. "Are you trying to wake someone out of an enchantment?"

"Yes, two people. Can you make the paste for me as soon as possible? I'll be there soon to collect it."

"I can do that."

"Great," I said. "Thanks."

When I ended the call, Felicity said, "Foxglove paste?"

"It's a traditional remedy for enchanted sleep. When applied to the eyelids of the sleeper, it wakes them up. Apparently. I've never actually had to use it before."

"You remember everything you learned at the Society?"

"I went to the Academy of Shadows. I've had this stuff floating around in my head from a young age."

Felicity frowned. "I've never heard of the Academy of Shadows."

"Not many people have. That reminds me, I need to call the Society and tell them that I'm not actually trapped in Faerie." I made the call to the London headquarters. I could probably have called the nearest American HQ, which happened to be in Massachusetts, but I preferred to go straight to the top. After all, my father was in the Inner Circle, so I should get something out of that other than attempts on my life.

A woman with an English accent answered and I asked for Thomas Harbinger. After confirming who I was, she put me through to him.

"Alec," he said in his usual gruff voice, "I was told you were lost in Faerie."

"I'm fine, Dad. You can call off the cavalry, if you were sending anyone here to help me."

"Well, actually, we weren't."

"Oh, okay." It felt great to be appreciated. The Society couldn't even be bothered to help me when they thought I was trapped in another realm.

"We knew you'd be all right, Son. You've been in worse scrapes before. By the way, how is your assistant getting on in her new job? She's brand new at this, so I thought it would be good experience for her to work for you."

"I know what you thought, Dad." *You thought you it was okay to send someone to spy on your son. Maybe you thought I would eventually confide in her about Paris and tell her more than I told the Society when I was interrogated with that damned truth collar around my neck.*

"Well, anyway, it's good to hear from you," he said. "I hear you're busy already. Good lad. Keep it up." He ended the call.

"That's nice," I told Felicity. "Even after you called them and told them I was trapped in Faerie, they weren't going to do anything to help."

"That's kind of good, though, because you said you didn't want them to help."

"I didn't."

"Well, then, it all turned out for the best."

"I guess so," I said, but I wasn't so sure. If I couldn't rely on the Society's help when I was in trouble, I was on my own out here. I had always had the Society to fall back on like a safety net, and when I was in Chicago, they couldn't do enough for me. My fall from grace had obviously changed that situation and now I was expected to fend for myself no matter what.

If the Society of Shadows wasn't going to offer me anything more than "we knew you'd be okay" platitudes, I might as well find people I could rely on and build a team of associates. There was Felicity, of course, and Mallory, when she was around and not chasing after a serial killer. I had no doubt that Leon would jump at the chance to help whenever he could. Maybe one day I'd trust the Blackwell sisters enough to call them part of my team, but for the moment, I wanted to keep them at arm's length; Devon's "vision," whether real or a parlor trick, had unnerved me.

Two hours later, we arrived in Dearmont and Felicity parked outside Blackwell Books. She ran inside to get the foxglove paste from the witches while I waited and watched the darkening sky through the Land Rover's windows. I hoped Mallory had those werewolves locked away. In about an hour's time, the curse would take effect and force them to become monsters. After the first turn, they would be able to shift at will and be in total control of themselves in wolf form, except for on the nights of the full moon when the shift would be uncontrollable and the beast within savage.

The RV stopped alongside me and the window buzzed down. Leon leaned over Michael so he could speak to me. "Hey, Alec, what do you want us to do?"

"I want you to go home," I said. "If I need you, I'll call, okay?"

He looked disappointed but nodded and said, "Okay, man." He disappeared from the window, which closed again. Michael gave me a nod and set off up the road.

Felicity returned a few minutes later with a jar of paste that was pale purple in color. She handed it to me as she got behind the wheel and I stashed it in the glove box.

"Those women look like they stepped out of the 1600s, but they seem nice enough," she said as she turned the Land Rover around and headed out of town toward the Robinson place.

"Yeah, they're very pleasant," I said, thinking of Devon's eyes rolling back in her head as she whispered, "*Empire of the Dead*." I really should tell Felicity about that sometime, but now wasn't that time.

Now was the time to save James Robinson and Sarah Silverman and kill the changelings that were trying to take over their lives.

Chapter 17

It was twilight when we arrived at the Robinson place. We left the Land Rover outside the gate and went inside on foot. I was carrying the sword, wrapped in its cloth shroud, and a flashlight that I hadn't turned on yet. Felicity had the foxglove paste in one hand and a dagger in the other, and candles and matches in her pocket. I'd considered bringing a shovel, in case James and Sarah were buried in one of the graves, but it seemed unlikely. The changelings wouldn't want to dig them up every night to feed, especially when the graveyard was a remote location anyway. I was sure that they'd want easier access to the bodies and had interred James and Sarah in the Robinson mausoleum.

We made our way across the lawn as quietly as we could, unlike the last time we were here when we'd tried to catch Changeling James's attention. This time, I wanted to get to the family cemetery before him and have time to wake up the sleeping beauties before he arrived.

The air had cooled and dark clouds had rolled in from the east, bringing with them a light, cold drizzle that wet our hair and clothes until we reached the shelter of the trees.

With the rain bouncing off the pine branches above our heads, we followed the narrow trail quickly to the iron-fenced graveyard. The gate stood open, but there didn't seem to be anyone around so we went into the enclosed, overgrown cemetery, fighting our way through the long grass and hawthorn vines to the mausoleum.

The structure's stone door opened easily, lending further credence to my theory that this was where James and Sarah were hidden. I turned on the flashlight and shone the beam inside the mausoleum. In the crypts along the walls, there were three coffins and two bodies. The bodies were those of James and Sarah. They were as still and quiet as the dead, but their pallor told me they were still alive, even if only barely.

"Hand me the paste," I whispered to Felicity. She passed it to me and I opened the jar. The paste had a pungent odor of rotting flowers that filled the mausoleum. I knelt next to James and applied the paste to his eyelids before doing the same for Sarah.

"Now what?" Felicity asked.

"Now we wait."

Outside, I heard movement in the grass.

"Someone's coming," Felicity whispered, unsheathing her dagger.

I unwrapped the sword, leaving the cloth on the stone floor of the mausoleum. The blade glowed brightly, illuminating the crypts, the two sleeping bodies, and the coffins in a ghostly blue luminescence.

I wasn't going to wait in this confined space for the changelings to come in here. I stepped out into the graveyard, sword held ready.

Changeling James stood within the open gate, staring at me. But his eyes didn't look like James's eyes anymore; they were yellow and lizard-like. Changeling Sarah stood behind him, a look of anger on her face. Like James, she had lizard eyes.

"What have you done?" Changeling James shouted at me. He took two steps forward, stared at the glowing sword in my hand, and stepped back toward the gate again. "We need to abandon these forms," he hissed to his companion. "There will be others."

"No, there really won't," I said, stepping toward them.

Changeling Sarah leapt at me in a hissing, clawing rage. I tried to swing the sword but she had me pinned against the stone wall of the mausoleum, making it hard to find the space the sword needed to strike. Her breath smelled of rotting meat as she hissed into my face.

I kicked her back with one boot, giving myself the room I needed to attack. She tried to lunge forward, but I swung the glowing blade in an upward arc, as if I were using a driver at a golf range, and the enchanted blade sliced up through her side and shoulder blade. She fell to the ground among the brambles and hawthorn vines. Howling in pain, she looked up at me with those reptilian eyes. Her entire body had changed now. She had assumed her true form. It was more snake-like than anything else, her body covered in scales that had a green hue, her mouth filled with needle-sharp fangs and a long forked tongue that flickered out from between her lips, tasting the air. Her scales shone slickly in the rain that was now coming down hard, turning the earth beneath my boots into mud.

Changeling James was running. He had fled through the open gate and was stumbling along the trail toward the house, casting glances over his shoulder at me as he ran.

"Felicity," I shouted toward the mausoleum. "I need to get to the house." I stepped through the brambles toward the changeling on the ground. I had to finish it. If it was allowed to live, it would go into hiding until it found another victim to imitate. I raised the sword above my head and swung it down with enough force to cut through its scales, skin, and heart. The creature collapsed, dead, its dark blood staining the wet ground.

Felicity appeared beside me, squinting against the rain that was streaking down the lenses of her glasses. I had told her to stay out of danger while I dealt with the changelings and to look after the bodies of James and

Sarah. She looked down at the reptilian creature lying in the mud. "Is that what they really look like?"

I nodded. "Yeah. The other one went to the house. You stay here and wait for James and Sarah to wake up. They'll be disoriented. The last thing they'll remember is walking through the woods at Dark Rock Lake, and maybe some vivid nightmares."

"Okay. Be careful, Alec."

"Always," I said, moving quickly through the open gate and on to the trail that led to the house. I ran over the wet dirt, the sword feeling light in my hand because of the adrenaline coursing through my veins. When I emerged from the trees and onto the lawn, my momentum sent me slipping on the slick grass. I lost my footing and landed on the ground, sliding on the wet lawn like a soccer player celebrating a goal. I scrambled to my feet and began running again, my clothing and skin soaked.

The front door to the house was open, all the lights inside burning bright. I entered the house and shouted, "Amelia!" I wasn't sure what the changelings plan was now that it was fleeing, but I needed to make sure Amelia and her husband were safe. I tried to remember his name. George. I was sure his name was George. I shouted, "George!"

The house was silent for a few seconds, but then I heard a crash and a scream from upstairs. I bounded up the stairs, trying to pinpoint the source of the sounds. A second scream sent me sprinting along the hallway, past framed family portraits, to a closed door. I kicked it open and rushed inside. There was no time for caution; I had to use surprise, speed, and aggression if I wanted an advantage over the changeling.

I barely had time to take in my surroundings as I entered the room because my vision focused on Amelia Robinson, crouched over the body of a man I presumed to be her husband. She was sobbing, "George," over and over. He was dressed in a dark suit and there was a ragged slash across the front of his neck and a stain on his shirt the color of red wine. Standing over him and his wife, long claws dripping blood, was the changeling. It turned toward me as I burst through the door and hissed, its tongue flickering in my direction.

My first thought was Amelia. I also remembered that there was a daughter, Georgia, somewhere in the house. I had to protect them. I reached for Amelia and grabbed her shoulder, pulling her away from her husband and out of reach of the changeling. She screamed, "No! George!" as she fell backward against the closet door. Her eyes went to the creature that had killed her husband—I was sure he was dead because of the amount of blood staining the carpet around his body—and she screamed again, but this time in terror.

The changeling leapt at me, tongue whipping out between razor-sharp fangs. Its weight and momentum sent us crashing to the floor, struggling against each other. But even as I'd fallen, I'd retained my tight grip on the sword. I smashed the hilt into the changeling's face, sending it scuttling away across the room, hissing angrily.

I got to my feet and walked toward the creature, the glow from my sword lighting the room in an eerie blue glow.

"Kill it!' Amelia Robinson sobbed. "Please kill it!"

The changeling was trapped against the wall with nowhere to run. I could see its body tensing, preparing to attack. I waited.

The reptilian creature sprang forward, claws slashing at me. I drove the point of the sword into its chest and pushed until it appeared out of the creature's back, running it through. The changeling went limp and became a dead weight, pulling the blade down. Its body slid off the blade and on to the carpet, lying there in a spreading pool of dark blood.

I turned to Amelia. "Where's your daughter?" I needed to know that Georgia Robinson was safe and I wanted to make Amelia think about something other than the fact that her husband was dead.

"I ... she ... she's at a friend's house." Her eyes were locked on her husband's dead body.

"Come with me." I grabbed her arm and led her from the room.

"Where are we going?" she asked as I took her to the stairs.

"I'm taking you to your son."

"Okay," she said, nodding. Her eyes were unfocused and I knew she was thinking about her husband and the creature that had killed him. She might be going into shock. I led her out into the rain and that seemed to bring her back to reality.

"I don't want to go into the woods," she said, pulling back from me as I led her across the lawn.

"Your son is there."

That seemed to placate her. She followed me along the trail toward the graveyard.

When we got there, I guided her around the gravestones to the mausoleum, keeping her away from the changeling's dead body lying in the mud.

Inside the mausoleum, Felicity had lit candles and placed them around the stone room. James and Sarah were sitting next to each other on the floor, both looking dazed. Their eyelids were stained purple from the foxglove paste.

I turned to Amelia. "This is your real son. The person who came back from the lake was an imposter." I wasn't going to give her a more detailed explanation right now, and I knew that she was in no mental state to listen to one. All she needed to know was that her son ... her real son ... was alive and well.

"James," she said, going to him.

"Mom." He hugged her. "I'm not sure what's happening, Mom."

"Don't worry about that now," I told them. James looked at me and the glowing sword in my hand, swallowed, and nodded.

I took Felicity to one side. "How are they?"

"Dazed, confused, and hungry."

"You stay here with them. I'm going to get the changeling's body out of the house and bury it along with the one out there." I pointed out of the door at the rain swept graveyard.

"How is she going to explain her husband's murder to the police?" Felicity whispered.

"I don't know, but she needs to keep us out of it. The Society is skilled at keeping its investigators out of prison for crimes they didn't commit, but I'm not sure they'd bother helping me now. They weren't even going to rescue me from Faerie, so I doubt they'd save me from a jail sentence. Anyway, I don't want to find out if they would or not, so help Amelia come up with a cover story and we'll hope that Sheriff Cantrell isn't the sharpest tool in the box."

Even as I said it, though, I had the feeling that Cantrell was a smart guy. I had nothing to base that assessment on other than a look of intelligence I'd noticed in his steely eyes as he'd looked out over Dearmont Lake in a photograph, but I was sure I was right about him.

My phone rang, the screen displaying Mallory's name. I answered it. "Hey, Mallory, how's it going?"

"Hello, Mr. Harbinger," said a deep male voice. "I have something here that I think is very valuable to you."

In the background, I heard Mallory shout, "Alec!"

"Shut up," the male voice said, "or I'll shoot you now." His voice was calm, calculated, and had an English accent. "Come to the McDermott Farm, Mr. Harbinger, and bring the box with you."

"What box?" I asked, feeling hot anger rise in me. I gripped the phone so hard that it dug painfully into my palm.

He had ended the call.

"Fuck!" I shouted, wanting to throw the phone against the wall and watch it shatter into a thousand pieces. If he hurt Mallory, I would kill him slowly, I was sure of that. I cursed myself for bringing her into this, for putting her in harm's way.

"Alec, what's wrong?" Felicity's face was full of concern.

"Someone has Mallory. I think he's from the Society."

"Oh my God. What can I do?"

"Call Leon and get him to get rid of the changeling bodies. He said he wanted to help, so now's his chance. Stay here with Amelia and come up with that story for the police. I need to go and kill someone." I turned to the door but stopped before I went outside. "Do you know anything about a box?"

She thought for a moment and then shrugged. "No, what kind of box?"

"I have no idea." I went out into the rain, rage building inside me, expressing itself in angry tears that mingled with the rain on my face.

CHAPTER 18

I RACED TO MCDERMOTT'S FARM, the Land Rover's wipers ticking like a clock as they swept rain from the windshield. The rain was coming down so hard now that it bounced off the road, forming a mist that hung in front of my headlights like a shroud over the blacktop. I felt so angry that I was determined to kill the man who had Mallory the moment I had the chance. I didn't care what he had to say or what he wanted: he was a dead man.

I saw a sign that said McDermott's Farm and skidded into a turn that pointed me in the right direction. I followed a dirt road past overgrown meadows and fields. Up ahead, through the rain, I could see the lights of the farm buildings. As I got closer, I saw that Mallory's orange Jeep Renegade was parked by the farmhouse, with a black car beside it that looked like a Bentley.

I skidded to a stop, parking the Land Rover in front of the Bentley and blocking its route out of here. No one was going anywhere without going through me first.

The dilapidated farmhouse had a rickety-looking wooden front porch that was sheltered from the rain by a sloped wooden roof. A porch light was on, casting a dull yellow glow. On the porch, there was a wooden bench that had once been white, but most of the paint had flaked away to reveal the bare wood beneath. Mallory sat on the bench.

Standing six feet away from her, a Winchester lever-action rifle in his hands, was a bearded man in an immaculate black suit, white shirt, and black tie. "Leave your weapons in the car, Mr. Harbinger," he called to me calmly.

I nodded and got out of the Land Rover. There was a dagger in a sheath tucked into the back of my jeans, beneath my shirt, but I didn't bring any visible weapons out with me.

"Who are you?" I asked him, walking toward the porch.

"That's close enough," he said when I was about twenty feet away. "And who I am isn't important. I go by the name of Tunnock, if knowing my name makes you feel happier. Now to the subject of our meeting. Did you bring the box?"

"What box?"

He shook his head disapprovingly. "Don't play games with me, Mr. Harbinger. I'm the one holding the gun. My employer told me that you have a box in your possession. I was told there'd be no point searching your house or office for it because you are much too clever to hide it in such an obvious place. My remit was to either recover the box or kill you. I tried the latter, but the two fools I sent to do the job never came back and here you are alive, so I can guess how that encounter went."

"If you mean those ogres, don't expect to see them ever again," I said.

"That's what I thought. So here I am in person, offering you a deal. The box for the girl. No one has to die here today."

"If this box is so important to your employer, then why isn't your employer here in person to deal with me?" I noticed Mallory trying to get my attention with her eyes. I glanced at her and she directed her gaze at her Jeep and nodded slightly toward the vehicle as if telling me to look there, too.

I looked over at the Jeep and felt my blood run cold. Timothy Ellsworth and a girl I assumed was Josie Carter were sitting in the backseat. Tunnock had made his move before Mallory had a chance to lock up the werewolves. I looked up at the rainy night sky. The full moon shone brightly behind dark clouds.

Twilight was passing and nightfall beginning. We were about to be joined by two werewolves and our chances of survival were slim.

"If you think your friends in the car are going to help you," Tunnock said, "you might as well think again. They know that if they come out here, this young lady's brains will be decorating the porch. Now, are you going to give me the box or not, Mr. Harbinger? Because I can just as easily kill you all. If the box is never found, my employer will be happy, just as long as you're dead so you can't use it."

I had no idea what box he was talking about, but I wasn't going to let him know that. My mind was racing, wondering what I was going to do when two werewolves came bursting out of the Jeep and Mallory and I were out here exposed.

I looked over at the Jeep. I couldn't see Timothy or Josie anymore, just two dark hulking shapes behind the windows. A loud bang rang out and the roof of the Jeep buckled upward as if struck by huge fists. The banging and pounding increased in pace.

Tunnock looked over at the Jeep, distracted for a split second by the noise. I reached back for the knife in my jeans and flicked it out of the sheath, dropping into a crouch as I did to steady myself for what I was about to do and present a smaller target to Tunnock if he managed to shoot in my direction. Adjusting my grip on the dagger so I held the tip of its blade between my forefinger and thumb, I brought it back to my ear before whipping my arm forward. The dagger flew through the air, spinning end over end until it embedded itself in Tunnock's chest.

It wasn't meant to kill him, just shock him long enough for me to reach him. I sprinted for the porch and dived at Tunnock, sending us both crashing through the farmhouse's front door. "Mallory," I shouted, "get in the Land Rover!"

I scrambled to my feet, meaning to grab Tunnock and drag him to the Land Rover, but he shook my hands off and pointed the Winchester at me. "Time to die, Mr. Harbinger."

I threw myself backward off the porch as he fired, feeling something hot rip into my right arm and spin me around slightly before I landed in the cold mud. Two big, furry shapes passed in front of me and I heard Tunnock scream and fire the rifle again, this time at the two werewolves.

Ignoring the pain in my arm, I sprinted for the Land Rover, meaning to get my rifle and silver-loaded shells out of the back. The shells wouldn't kill a werewolf; the only way to do that is to drive silver through the creature's heart and a shotgun isn't powerful enough. The silver shells stunned them, though, and my usual method of killing a werewolf was to stun it with the shotgun and then drive a silver dagger through the creature's heart.

The back of the Land rover was already open and Mallory stood there with my shotgun in hand. She passed it to me. "Fully loaded with werewolf stunners."

"What would I do without you?" I asked as I took the gun and went back to the house.

Tunnock must have run into one of the rooms because neither he nor the werewolves were by the front door anymore.

Brandishing the shotgun, I stepped into the house and saw the path that Tunnock must have taken. To the left, the kitchen door was open, and the dust on the floor had been disturbed by shoes and huge paws. I went into the kitchen, gun leveled in front of me. There was nobody there, just a kitchen table collecting dust and cobwebs....

Then I heard a scream and a growl coming from an open door on the rear wall of the kitchen. I went to it and saw wooden steps leading down into darkness. The basement. This was where Mallory was going to lock up the wolves for the night. Tunnock had led them down there.

I closed the door and locked it.

CHAPTER 19

AS I STEPPED OFF THE porch, I slipped in the mud, but managed to stay on my feet. Mallory rushed over and put her arms around my shoulders, guiding me to the Land Rover. Now that the adrenaline had burnt out of my system, the pain in my right arm flared. Blood was seeping through my shirt and trickling down over my hand.

"We need to get you to a hospital," Mallory said.

"No, no hospital. They report gunshot wounds to the police and I don't want to have to explain where this came from."

She led me to the passenger side of the Land Rover and I climbed in. As she got in the driver's seat, Mallory said, "I'll use the medical supplies at your house to patch you up." She backed away from Tunnock's Bentley and spun the Land Rover around in the mud so it was facing the dirt road out of here.

"The medical stuff's all packed in boxes. I'm not sure where it is," I said.

"I unpacked everything for you while you were gone."

"You did? I was only joking when I said…."

"Yeah, I know you were, but I didn't mind doing it for you."

I grinned at her. I probably looked terrible covered in rain, mud, and blood, but I knew Mallory didn't care. "Thanks."

We bumped along on the dirt road. Mallory put on the windshield wipers, but by the time we hit the highway, the rain had died.

"Tunnock," she said. "Is he…?"

I nodded grimly. "Yeah, he decided to use himself as werewolf bait and lead Timothy and Josie into the basement." I paused and then said, "See, you always get the easy jobs. All you had to do was get the werewolves into the basement and you let Tunnock do it for you."

She shot me a disapproving look.

"Too soon?" I asked.

"Yeah, too soon. The guy died."

"That's his own fault. He should never have threatened to hurt you."

She went quiet for a few moments before asking, "Who do you think he was? And what's this box he was talking about?"

"I have no idea. Whatever it is, someone thinks I have it, and they're willing to kill me because of it."

My phone rang. It was Leon. "Hey, Alec," he said when I answered. "That job is all taken care of. We buried them in the cemetery behind the mausoleum."

"Thanks," I said.

"Are you okay? You sound tired."

"I'm fine. How is James?"

"He's confused about what happened. Felicity is talking with him and Sarah now. Then Mrs. Robinson is going to call the police and tell them that she found her husband like that and she has no idea how it happened."

"That's probably the safest story," I said. "It's easier for her to stick to that than a fabricated lie with a lot of false details. Leon, you did a really good job tonight. Thanks."

"No problem, man. If you ever need me again, you know the number."

I ended the call and sat back in my seat, looking through the windshield at the stars and the full moon as we drove to my place.

Mallory saw me stargazing and said, "It certainly is beautiful around here."

"Yeah," I said, nodding. "It certainly is."

* * *

An hour later, I was sitting at my kitchen table while Mallory poked my wound with a stainless steel probe. As soon as we'd arrived home, I'd taken a long, hot shower to wash away all the mud and blood and dirt that covered my body. My muscles ached and the wound in my right arm throbbed.

Mallory had showered after me and was now wearing only a gray t-shirt and pink panties while she examined my wound. I was dressed in a fresh white T-shirt and a pair of boxers.

"The bullet went straight through," she said. "It isn't too bad."

"That's easy for you to say; it isn't your arm that's wounded."

She poured some iodine onto a cotton ball and dabbed it onto my arm. "Does that sting?"

"No," I lied.

"Liar." She applied a dressing to the wound and said, "There. Good as new."

I moved my arm experimentally, grimacing at the pain that flared all the way to my shoulder.

"It'll take some time," Mallory said, "but it will heal eventually."

"Thanks. Maybe you should drive me around for a while so I can rest it."

She threw a cotton ball at my face. "I'm not your personal chauffeur. If you want a driver, get your lovely assistant to do it."

I threw the cotton ball back at her. "Why would I do that when I've got you?"

"Because if Felicity was driving you around, you could stare at her legs like you do all time anyway."

"I do not."

"Yes, you do." She poked the dressing on my arm playfully.

"Ow, quit it, that really hurt," I said, putting a pained expression on my face that was obviously exaggerated.

"I bet you wouldn't tell Felicity to quit it." She poked it again and laughed.

"Of course I would," I poked my finger at her stomach but she moved away quickly and backed into the living room. Putting on a high voice, she said, "Oh, Mr. Harbinger, may I poke your wound?" Her voice deepened and she said, "Of course, Felicity, poke it as much as you like."

Laughing, I stood up and said, "That's it. The final straw. You are going down." I grabbed a cushion from the sofa and held it in my left hand, ready to throw at her.

She adopted the high voice again. "Oh, Mr. Harbinger, you're so big and strong."

I threw the cushion and Mallory karate-chopped it away. But as soon as I'd thrown it, I'd also jumped forward at her. I grabbed her waist and we tumbled to the floor, me on top of her.

I looked down into her hazel eyes and suddenly I wanted her more than I'd ever wanted any other woman. She looked up at me with a hungry expression and lifted her head to kiss me.

Nothing else mattered in that moment; not the fact that the Society had banished me, or that I was indebted to the Lady of the Forest, or that someone was trying to kill me. The only thing that mattered was my bond with Mallory and its physical expression in a kiss.

When our lips parted and we looked into each other's eyes, the atmosphere in the room had changed from humorous to serious.

"Alec," Mallory whispered, "let's go to bed."

"Sure, but nothing is going to happen, okay?"

She pouted. "Why not?"

"Because I don't want you to feel afraid tonight. I don't want you to think about the shadows or ghosts of the past."

She nodded. "That sounds perfect."

Later, when we were lying in bed next to each other in the dark, she said, "Don't forget, you owe me a new Jeep."

"What? How do you figure that?"

"Those werewolves wouldn't have been in the back seat if I hadn't been doing your job for you."

"Doing my job for me?"

"Hell yeah, doing your job while you were taking a moonlit stroll in the woods."

"I was fighting changelings."

"Well, whatever you were doing, that doesn't change the fact that my car got wrecked while performing your duties."

"I'll get you a Society of Shadows expense claim form," I said, jokingly. "But somehow, I don't think they'll buy you a new Jeep."

"Ugh! They suck."

"Yeah, they do." I rolled over to face her. "I thought that maybe after work tomorrow, I'd have a party here to celebrate my first case closed in Dearmont. It'd be a housewarming party, too."

She smiled. "Sounds great. Am I invited?"

"Of course. Everybody who helped out is invited. You, Felicity, Leon, and Michael."

"What about the witches?"

"Nah, I don't think so. They're probably not partygoers anyway."

"You never know. Looks can be deceiving."

"I think I'll stick to the people I mentioned," I said.

She looked at me closely. "You're worried about what Devon Blackwell saw in her vision, aren't you? About you being under an enchantment. That's why those witches freak you out so much; you're afraid of what they said."

"Well, I don't like to think that part of my mind has been locked away behind a magical door. Seeing those witches reminds me of it."

"Don't worry," she said, snuggling against me, "we'll figure it out somehow."

After Mallory had fallen asleep and was breathing deeply next to me, I lay looking at the ceiling and wondering what had happened in Paris that I couldn't remember.

It was a long time before I fell asleep.

CHAPTER 20

THE FOLLOWING MORNING, MALLORY AND I drove to McDermott Farm. The sky was overcast with gray clouds, but at least there was no rain. When we got to the farm, Tunnock's Bentley was gone. I wasn't surprised; whoever he was working for made sure they left no trail behind.

Mallory inspected the remains of her Jeep Renegade while I went into the house through the broken front door. I had clothing belonging to Timothy and Josie that they had given to Mallory the night before, after being told that turning into werewolves would destroy the clothes they were wearing.

There were more tracks in the dust than there had been yesterday, a couple of sets of boot prints that led to the basement door, and then away again. Someone had probably come in here to find Tunnock, heard the werewolves in the basement and then left again. They'd probably come back at some point to remove what was left of his body.

I unlocked the door, expecting to find Timothy and Josie sitting at the top of the stairs waiting to be released, but there was no one there. Voices drifted up from the darkness below. The two were chatting with each other. I went down the wooden steps and found them sitting naked against the wall, talking. They both looked up at me with sheepish faces, as if I had caught them doing something they shouldn't.

"Hey, you two, how's it going?" I asked.

"Fine," Timothy said. "So I guess we're werewolves, huh?"

"Yeah." I tossed them the clothes. "Get dressed and we'll talk about it on the way home." I went back upstairs to let them get dressed in private.

Outside, Mallory was trying to flatten some of the dents in the Jeep's bodywork with her fist.

"You need a mechanic for that," I told her. I went over and looked at the damage. The back window was smashed and the roof had taken a pummeling, but it wasn't too bad considering two werewolves had broken out of there.

"And what am I going to tell said mechanic?" she asked.

"Tell him you have a couple of rowdy kids."

"Very funny."

Timothy and Josie came out of the house, blinking at the morning light. Josie was about Timothy's age and had ginger hair and freckles. They both came over to the Jeep. "We want to apologize," Timothy said to Mallory. "We know we did that to your car and we want to make it up to you. We'll pay for the repairs."

"Thanks. Are you sure you can afford it?" Mallory asked.

"Yeah," Josie said. "Timothy works at the game store and I have a job in the coffee shop. Neither of us spends much because we don't go out much."

"Sounds like you two have been getting to know each other," I said.

"We're very alike," Timothy said. "I don't just mean the werewolf thing, either. We both live with our moms and look after them and we like a lot of the same movies and books."

"That's great," I said, wondering if I should advertise my werewolf security work as a matchmaking service. "Let's get out of here. You guys ride with me and I'll explain what I know about werewolves. There's some stuff that's pretty cool. But first, I have a question for both of you."

They looked at me expectantly.

"Who wants to come to my party tonight?"

They grinned. They seemed like good kids, and I liked them. Maybe my party could be their first date together.

As I got into the Land Rover, Mallory looked at me, smiling and shaking her head.

"What?" I asked innocently.

"You make out like you're some tough guy, but you're actually quite sentimental."

"You know me," I said, starting the engine. "I love a good romance."

* * *

The party was in full swing by eight. I'd set out snack food on the kitchen table along with beer, wine, and soda. Mallory had programmed her iPod to play a selection of pop music after deciding that the music on my phone wasn't suitable because there was way too much classic rock.

At eight o' clock, Felicity was on the sofa, a glass of white wine in her hand, talking with Leon and Michael. Mallory was chatting with Timothy and Josie and a Taylor Swift song was drifting out of the iPod speaker. I'd been moving from one group to another, butting into conversations and telling everyone about my bullet wound.

The doorbell rang and I frowned at Mallory. "Did you invite anyone else?"

She shook her head.

I went to the door and opened it. Sheriff Cantrell and his redheaded deputy stood outside.

"Sheriff," I said, sounding as surprised as I felt.

"Mr. Harbinger?" he asked. "Alec Harbinger?"

"Yes."

"May we come in?"

"Yeah, sure. If it's about the noise…."

He stepped into the living room, seeming to fill the room with his bulk, followed by the deputy, who looked even more gorgeous in real life than she had in the photo I'd seen on the internet.

"It isn't about the noise, it's about this," the sheriff said. He showed me a package he was holding. It was about the size of a toaster and wrapped in brown paper.

Mallory paused the music. Everyone looked from the sheriff to me.

"What is it?" I asked him.

He sighed as if I was trying his patience. "I have no idea what it is. I'm here to tell you that the Dearmont police station is not your personal postal service."

"I'm aware of that," I said. I wanted to add, "Yet here you are with a package," but stopped myself.

"Is that right?" He looked at me with his steely eyes. "Well, let me tell you a story. Three weeks ago, Gus, the town's mailman comes into the station and he tells me he has a package to deliver, but there's no address on it except 'Dearmont, Maine, USA.' He wanted to know if I recognized the name on it. I told him I didn't. So imagine my surprise when, three weeks later, the person named on the package moves into town." He thrust the package into my arms. I winced when the wound on my right arm flared.

I looked down at the address written in blue pen across the top of the package. *Alec Harbinger, Dearmont, Maine, USA.* The postage stamps were French.

"Don't ask people to mail you something and address it to the town," Cantrell said. "Things like that usually end up on my desk and I don't like it."

"I promise you, it won't happen again," I said. "You really didn't have to bring it here in person. I could have come to the station to collect it. You could have called me, or come by my office. I work…."

"I know where you work," he said. "And I know what you do. I came here tonight because I wanted to take a look at you and where you live. I have a feeling that you and I are going to be butting heads, and I like to know my enemy."

"Enemy? That's a little harsh, don't you think?"

Without answering me, he turned on his heels and left the house. The deputy followed but I said, "Wait, please. What does he mean by 'enemy?' I haven't done anything wrong."

She looked at me with a pleading look in her eyes. "Please don't take it personally, Mr. Harbinger. It isn't who you are that makes him mad. It's what you are."

"What?"

"Amy!" the sheriff shouted from the driveway.

"I have to go," she said, turning away from me and going out onto the driveway. The sheriff's patrol car was parked at the curb, and the sheriff was glaring at her through the driver's window.

I went back into the living room with the package and placed it on the kitchen table next to the snacks.

Everyone gathered around it. "It's from France," Mallory said. "Do you think someone in Paris sent it to you?"

I sighed. "Yeah, I do, but there are two things very wrong about this package. Three week ago, when this was sent, I was in Paris and hadn't yet been sent to Dearmont, so how can this be addressed to me here?"

We all thought about that for a few seconds but nobody had an answer.

"What's the second thing?" Felicity asked.

"The handwriting on the package," I said. "It's mine."

Mallory leaned in to take a closer look. "Oh my God, it is yours. You sent this package to yourself?"

"Apparently, I sent it to myself, to a town I'd never heard of."

"You don't remember sending it?" Leon asked.

I shook my head.

"So open it, man," he said.

I went to the kitchen drawer and took out a sharp knife. Returning to the table, I cut through the cardboard and opened the package. Inside, there were shredded strips of French newspaper that had been used as packing material. I thrust my hand into it and contacted something solid that felt like metal. I brought it out and held it up to the light.

It was an ornate box made of silver and gold and inscribed with Egyptian hieroglyphs. It had no latch or keyhole or anything else that suggested it could be opened. I had no idea what it was but I had mailed it to myself from Paris before the Society even decided to send me to Dearmont.

I placed it on the table, where it glinted in the light.

"So," I said, "this must be the box that someone wants to kill me for." It was pretty, sure, but it looked insignificant sitting there on the table next to the party snacks. It certainly didn't look like it was worth dying for.

I needed some air. I grabbed a bottle of beer and went out into the yard, looking up at the starry sky while I tried to think straight. Why the hell was this box so important?

Felicity came out with a bottle of beer of her own and smiled at me. "Hey, want some company?"

"Yeah, sure. I was just thinking about that damned box. I don't know what it is or why it's important but I must have known something about it when I was in Paris because I mailed it here. I have no idea how I even got my hands on it in the first place."

"I'll do some research. If it's some kind of artifact, there'll be a record of it somewhere."

"Yeah," I said, looking at the stars again. "It's been a hell of a couple of days, huh?"

ADAM J. WRIGHT

"A couple of days for you, a week for me. You were in Faerie for five days, remember?"

"Oh, yeah. So how was the first week in your new job?" I looked at her and grinned.

"Well I can't say it was boring, that's for sure. Scary, dangerous, and worrying, yes. Boring, no."

"Worrying?"

"Yeah, mainly waiting for you to get back from Faerie, not knowing if you were okay or injured, or dead."

"Well, it's nice to be worried about."

Felicity didn't say anything and I couldn't read her eyes behind the reflection of the moon in her glasses.

"You ready for week two?" I asked her.

"Oh, hell yeah."

"I do have one request for when I arrive at the office tomorrow," I said.

One eyebrow arched above her glasses. "What's that?" she asked suspiciously.

"I'd like some more of those apple bakes."

"Would you, indeed?"

"Any kind of baked goods will do, actually."

She nodded slowly. "Okay, I think I can manage that."

I grinned. "We're going to make a great team." I raised my bottle. "Here's to many cases in the future."

Felicity smiled. "I'll drink to that." She clinked her bottle against mine and we drank our beers while looking up at the bright stars.

Maybe this sleepy town wasn't so bad after all.

THE END

LOST SOUL

BURIED MEMORY

DEAD GROUND

To join the Harbinger P.I. mailing list and get news of new releases in the series:

http://eepurl.com/bRehez

CPSIA information can be obtained
at www.ICGtesting.com
Printed in the USA
BVHW030819010319
541541BV00001B/14/P